EXPLICIT EROTIC SEX STORIES

This book includes: Taboo Sex Stories for Adults and Dirty Short Stories. Lesbian, BDSM, Threesome, Gangbang, Romantic and Forbidden Desires And Much More...

Jenna Grey

© **Copyright 2020 Jenna Grey**
All rights reserved.

The content contained within this book may not be reproduced, duplicated or transmitted without direct written permission from the author or the publisher.

Under no circumstances will any blame or legal responsibility be held against the publisher, or author, for any damages, reparation, or monetary loss due to the information contained within this book. Either directly or indirectly.

Legal Notice:
This book is copyright protected. This book is only for personal use. You cannot amend, distribute, sell, use, quote or paraphrase any part, or the content within this book, without the consent of the author or publisher.

Disclaimer Notice:
Please note the information contained within this document is for educational and entertainment purposes only. All effort has been executed to present accurate, up to date, and reliable, complete information. No warranties of any kind are declared or implied. Readers acknowledge that the author is not engaging in the rendering of legal, financial, medical or professional advice. The content within this book has been derived from various sources. Please consult a licensed professional before attempting any techniques outlined in this book.

By reading this document, the reader agrees that under no circumstances is the author responsible for any losses, direct or indirect, which are incurred as a result of the use of information contained within this document, including, but not limited to, — errors, omissions, or inaccuracies.

TABLE OF CONTENTS

Dirty Short Stories

Celina and her "Fifty Shades of Grey"..........................1
Two Hot Student Girls Work one Cock... Yes Master! 14
John and His Hot Step-Sisters: Family Business 31
Betrayal and the Sexy Revenge 42
Lydia and her first Party with a bang! 58
Sub Zero...77
Craving Pleasure 90

Taboo Sex Stories

Complete Bliss..124
Frat Party 160
Painting Love..192
Wheel Of Motion 222
Witty Sunday 241

DIRTY SHORT STORIES

Explicit and Exciting Erotic Sexy Stories for Adults, Taboo Collection: Threesome, Gangbang, BDSM, Step Fantasy And Much More...

Jenna Grey

Celina and her "Fifty Shades of Grey"

Celina was sat on the couch with John and Dean. They all went to the same college but became friends when they started sharing a house together. Celina was "one of the boys". She watched football, drank beer, and used foul language. They were all good friends and often had nights in together watching films. Today was no exception. They had been watching some scary movie that they found rather boring and were just chatting when "Fifty Shades of Grey" came on. None of them had seen it before so they left it on. When they went into the room with all the toys in, Celina commented that her collection was better and then laughed. The boys looked at her with raised eyebrows.

"What? I have my own toys, can't a girl pleasure herself?" She asked.

They boys just shrugged and mumbled inaudibly. She laughed at them.

"Well I am single, and I have to get my satisfaction somehow! It's not like either of you have ever offered to help a girl out!" She commented

They both were taken aback and looked a little put out. She sat there with an expectant expression on her face.

"Well?"

John was first to answer. "If I had known you felt that way, I may have mentioned it before!"

Celina rolled her eyes at him and looked to Dean, "Have you got anything to say?" she mocked him.

"Let's get it on!" he replied. At that point he pulled her on to him and kissed her. She pulled back, surprised, then shrugged her shoulders and resumed the kiss. John sat back not knowing what to do. He had wished that he had instigated the proceedings as was now sat there like a spare wheel.

John watched as Celina straddled Deans legs. She was rubbing herself along the seam of his jeans. Her hands were on the couch behind him and she had her tongue in his mouth. His hands were on her waist, pushing her back and forth on his crotch, making his erection bigger as he did. He lifted his hand up to her breasts and began to rub them through the material of her top. He watched as her nipples hardened and poked through the thin material. John took hold of her arm and pulled her across the couch towards him and she went willingly. She did the same to john, teasing him with her tongue and getting him hard by rubbing herself on him.

She pushed herself off him and stood up in front of them. She took off her top and dropped her skirt to the floor. They both watched as she stripped for them, both rubbing themselves through their jeans. When she was naked, she put her hands on her hips and looked at them both. They shifted themselves about of the sofa and she knelt on the sofa with her head towards John.

She undid his jeans and pulled out his cock. She grasped it in her hand and began to rub him up and down. She felt hands on her butt and realised that dean was stroking it. He planted kisses on both cheeks before licking her knotted hole.

"Hmmmm" she responded to his touch. He pushed his tongue inside her arsehole and then removed it. He then pushed a finger into it so he could penetrate her further and she pushed back against him.

She was playing with John's cock before dipping her head and taking him into her mouth. He groaned as she slid her lips down his entire length. She removed him from her mouth and began to lick the underside, flicking her tongue over the head and back down. She licked his ball sack before taking him back into her mouth and started to suck him off.

Her head flew up and down his large cock and she took it all. As she drew her lips up, she sucked hard. John was loving the feeling of her mouth around is cock. He placed his hands on her head to encourage her to suck more. He was surprised that she could take all his cock as he was long and quite thick around the girth. She did not struggle to reach the base and she slowly started to fondle his balls at the same time.

Dean was pumping his fingers in and out of her butt and she pushed back to meet him every time. He pulled his finger out and lowered his head to lick her pussy. He slipped his tongue inside her and began to lap at her fold. He bent down further to suck on her clitoris. This made her push back harder and he had to move to keep it in his mouth. His tongue swirled round the little bud and her moans were getting louder.

As she moaned the vibrations caused by her vocal cords, stimulated John more and he was getting close to cumming. He did not want to be the first to, and he did not want to cum in her mouth. He lifted her off him and asked her to turn round. Dean was still sucking her clit when she stood up and pulled away from him. He looked confused before he realised, she was turning round. He quickly stood and removed his trousers, before sitting back down.

Celine put her head in Deans lap whilst John knelt behind her. He began to play with Deans cock, and she felt her pussy lips being parted and John slipped his large cock inside her. She arched her back as he entered her before leaning forward again to take Dean in her mouth. He was as long as John, but his girth was wider. She had more trouble taking all of him in her mouth but was determined to do the same for both men. She massaged his balls whilst her head bobbed on his dick and he sat back to enjoy the feeling. He did not put his hands on her head, instead he cupped her breast and played with her nipples. They responded by getting hard again and she softly moaned against his cock.

John took hold of her hips and slowly began to slide in and out of her. He liked how his dick glistened with her juice. He took it slow as he did not want to cum right away, but she felt so tight around him. He found that he could not push all the way in, and it built his confidence, thinking he was too big for her to take him all. As he pushed in, she rocked back, and his balls slapped against her pussy. It was such a satisfying noise that he pushed harder each time to make it again.

Celine was loving being tended to by 2 men. It had always been a favourite of hers. She hoped that this might now turn into a regular thing if the boys were not too jealous about sharing her. If they were, she could always fuck them individually. She loved the feel of a cock in her mouth and one in her pussy. She like that fact that both men were long and had good girth, so she would feel full of them inside her. She began to rock back on John faster, not caring if he came quick as it would mean he would last longer later.

Dean watched as she bobbed her head on his dick, he had never really thought of Celina this way but now that the opportunity has arisen, he would be more than happy to help her out in future. He had been going through a bit of a dry spell himself so it was good knowing he could be with her when the need arose.

John could feel his balls tighten as his climax got near and he tried to hold back as long as he could. He felt the warmth spread through his groin and he increased his pace to meet hers. He gripped her hips tight as he got nearer to ejaculating, his body stiffened as his seed shot out inside her. He pumped her full until he had nothing left to give. He pulled out of her and collapsed onto the couch; his body covered in sweat.

Celine felt john erupt into her as her muscles clamped around his cock. She knew he would cum quickly as he had not been with a woman in a while and she was pleased that she had milked him. He plans for the rest of the night depended on it. As soon as he pulled out, she stopped sucking Deans cock and turned round. She straddled his lap and speared herself on his tool. She held him in place as her pussy adjusted to the bigger dick then she began rocking on his cock. Dean grasped both of her breasts and played with them both. He brushed his thumbs over her nipples and then licked each of them in turn. He loved watching nipples react to stimulus as they shrivelled and poked out more when they were erect. He allowed her to set the pace, but he thrust up to meet her as she lowered herself onto his cock.

Celine slipped her hand between them and began to rub on her clit, sending her body into shivers. She leant forward and kissed Dean who immediately reciprocated it. Their tongues entwined and wrestled, sending sparks between them. Her clitoral stimulation set a chain reaction off and her pussy muscles started to spasm around his penis. She felt the warm tingle spread through her body and she threw her head back and groaned as her orgasm rippled through her. The spasms in her pussy sent waves of pleasure through Dean and his balls clenched. She bounced up and down on him getting faster and faster until her body froze then juddered as her climax hit.

Dean felt her go rigid and her pussy tightened around him. She milked his cock and he began to unload within her. His cum squirted inside her and flooded her, it mixed with her own juice and dribbled out of his crotch. He looped his arms under hers and put his hands on her shoulders, pulling her down onto him and he emptied his sack. They collapsed on the couch together, all of them breathing hard and sweating.

After a few minutes they had recovered a bit from their little session.

"So, boys, did you enjoy the warm-up?" she enquired.

They looked round her at each other and asked what she meant.

"Well, she replied now that you have both cum and emptied your sacks, we can crack on with the main session" They looked confused at first, then they both agreed.

"Good," she said, "as you may have noticed I like my butt played with and I want one of you in my arse while the other is in my pussy!" She looked at them in turn. "Which one of you wants the top bunk?"

Before john had had chance to even think about the question, Dean had answered. "I want top bunk!"

"Ok, now we have that established, I need to get you both hard again. With that she stood up and walked over to the coffee table and dragged it over to the sofa. She turned and sat on it, so her bum was just on the edge. She spread her legs wide and began to stroke herself. The boys watched with their hands on their dicks slowly rubbing them. She lifted her fingers to her mouth and spat on them then returned them to her clit. She started off slowly circling the little bud before gradually speeding up. She gave her pussy a few little slaps then shoved 2 fingers inside her. She squelched as she fingered herself and the mixture of cum squirted out from between her legs. She soon made herself cum and as she looked over to the boys, they were both fully hard. She smiled at herself before standing up and walking over towards John.

She made him lay down on the couch and again straddled him. She guided his hard cock into her pussy and then stretched her legs back behind her and parted them. Dean could see her arse hole above her cock filled pussy and he could not wait to get in there. He spat on his hand and rubbed the fluid into his cock before laying on top of her and slipping his cock inside. He could feel John's cock in her pussy, and they spent a few minutes getting accustomed to the feel. The only person who had done this before was Celina and she talked them through the best way accomplish this challenge. Between the boys they worked out the best rhythm for them and then began to fuck her properly. As one of them pulled back the other would thrust forwards like 2 pistons in an engine. They adjusted the speed, constantly asking if that was ok with Celina. When they were all comfortable, they picked up the pace.

Celina started groaning immediately and the boys knew that she would cum multiple times whilst doing this. She felt completely full and could feel each of the boy's twitch and move as they prepared for each thrust. She was so happy that they had agreed to this as it was her favourite of all positions. She got maximum satisfaction and stimulation and the boys would be able to feel what the other was doing. As the boys fucked her, they could feel the other persons cock and as they rubbed together, it caused an unusual but nice sensation. That, combined with the clenching of her muscles, had them both getting near to another orgasm. Each of them desperate not to cum before she did. Neither of them thought that would really be an issue as she was now screaming the house down that she was cumming. They sped up their thrusts and drove their cocks into her harder and harder.

She felt them increase the sped they were going, and she could feel the warmth spread through her body again. She tingled all over and even her hair felt that it was tingling. She bit down on John's shoulder as wave after wave flowed through her body. She shuddered as her climax hit and the boys felt it too. She held them both tight within her as her body spasmed and then she flopped down onto John. The boys were now essentially fucking the others cock and they rocked harder to reach their own climax. It was not long before they both filled her up with their seeds and collapsed into a pile on the sofa.

All 3 were drawing deep breaths as they parted, and as Dean climbed off Celina, she felt the cum run between her legs. She pushed herself off John and stood up.

"I am going for a shower now, then I am going to bed!" She sounded quite stand offish and then she added "so, same time tomorrow?" then turned and walked off.

Two Hot Student Girls Work one Cock... Yes Master!

Jessica and violet were best friends. They had been in boarding school together for 5 years and they were both naughty. They always got into trouble together and were forever being sent to the year head regarding their discipline. He was a bit of a push over and despite them telling him they would be better, they never changed. They were terrible. This time, however, they had gone too far! They were being sent to the headmaster and he was not an easy person to get round.

The pair realised how much trouble they were in and were actually worried about having their parents called in. They had come up with a plan to lessen the punishment and they hoped it would work. The pair had taken their time getting ready for the appointment with him and were dressed in their uniform but had adjusted it to become a little sexier. Being 17, they were of legal age but due to difficulties in previous years they had been held back a year. They were both blond, Jessica was more endowed than her counterpart. Violet had a bigger backside though.

They walked through the halls of the school when everyone else had been at dinner and arrived at his office. Jessica knocked on the door and they were told to enter. Jessica opened the door and they walked in. The stood before his desk and placed their hands behind their backs. They remained quiet until he spoke to them.

"You pair will be the death of me, you have endangered your friends and the reputation of this school with your stupid pranks. You both think you are funny, and clever but you are not. You are pathetic and silly. Your hairbrained schemes are a mockery of our great traditions, and I am lost as to what to do with you!" Master Williams berated them. He was a tall man of great stature, and had an air about him, which commanded respect. He was a very handsome man, looking like Sean Connery with a voice to match.

"What am I to do?" He asked, and the girls looked down at their feet. "Have you nothing to say for yourselves?" he queried. When they remained quiet, he added, "Well I will just have to call your parents in for a meeting!"

"No" The girls said in unison, "Please don't do that Sir!" They pleaded with him.

"There must be something we can do for you Sir?" Violet asked?

He lifted his gaze towards her, and she stood twirling her hair around her finger. He looked at how they were dressed, and his face went red with anger.

"Even the way you wear our uniform is an afront to everything we hold dear!" He marched around his huge desk and grabbed Violets collar, as he pulled it to make his point, the buttons on her shirt popped off. She clasped her arms across her chest to cover herself.

Jessica's quick thinking kicked in and she shouted, "Sir, what have you done? You have assaulted my friend and tore her clothes like a rabid animal! My parents will hear about this!" She dramatically turned away covering her eyes and he backed off, nearly falling over his desk as he did so.

"No, No, No, Please, this is just a mis-understanding!" He stammered now, and she knew she had him just where she wanted him.

"But Sir, I have to report this! My friend is traumatised by this event and I think she will need counselling to help her overcome this." Jessica laid it on thick, making Master Williams feel uncomfortable.

"What is it you want? I will give you anything?" He asked of her.

Jessica thought for a few moments before answering. "We want for you to mark all of our work and give us top marks, we want to be allowed of campus whenever we want, we don't need money, so what else can we think of?" She tapped her finger against her lip while she thought about what else they wanted.

"Oh yeah, we want you!" she added.

"What do you mean?" He asked.

"Well Sir, we are to young women in our experimental years, and while we are cooped up here, we cannot go out and spread our proverbial wings! This means, that whenever we want to, either on our own or together, we can leave our lessons, come to you and play!" She said coyly.

He looked between the girls to see if they were serious and when he realised, they were, he began to say no.

Jessica raised her voice over his and said, "Or we could go and report this assault to our parents, the other teachers, the board of governors, and the media. This would mean that you would lose your job, get sued and probably never work again!"

He looked at her in disbelief, opening and closing his mouth before he dropped his shoulders in defeat and agreed to their terms.

Violet looked over at her friend with utter admiration and shone a beaming smile towards her.

She then turned to Master Williams, who looked downtrodden, and walked over to him. She placed her arms around his head and pulled him into her bust. "There, there, Sir, don't be sad. Just think, you get to spend so much time with us hot girls." She giggled.

He turned his head into her chest and nuzzled between her breasts. "That's its Sir, let yourself go!"

He wrapped his arms around her waist and pulled her closer to him. He began kissing her cleavage and made his way up to her collar bone then to her mouth. He placed his mouth over hers and she parted her lips for him. She slipped her tongue inside his mouth and began to swirl it around.

Jessica went to the door and turned the latch. She did not want her plan ruined by someone walking in on them. She turned back to watch the scene unfolding, just in time to see him remove her friend's blouse. She smiled knowing that she would soon be in on the action and that her plan had gone so smoothly. She walked back over to the desk and went around the far side, where she climbed up on the leather surface. She crawled across it and placed her hands on his shoulders. He jumped in reaction, but she soon put him at ease as she began kissing his earlobes and nibbling them gently.

Violet had her boobs out of her bra now and he was holding each one in his hands. He roughly rubbed them with his fingers and watched how the young pert skin reacted. He bent his head down and licked her swollen globes, sending shivers through her body. Violet lowered her hands to his groin and began stroking his cock through his trousers. He reacted quickly and she felt him harden to her touch.

Jessica pulled them apart and told him to lay on the desk. He sat on the edge then lowered himself, so he was flat. Violet went back to his crotch and unzipped him, before placing a hand inside and pulling out his cock. Jessica was knelt with her knees either side of his head and she flashed her white knickers at him. He stared up at the gusset and liked his lips. She hooked her thumbs in the strings at the sides of her underwear before lowering them and taking them off. She lipped them across his nose before dropping them on the floor.

He watched her put a hand between her legs and begin circling her own clitoris. Her sweet smell wafted down towards him and he inhaled deeply. He desperately wanted to taste her, but she would make him wait. She rubbed her bud hard and moans started to escape her. She was very aroused, and she came quickly by her own hand. Her juice dripping from her onto his face. He stuck out his tongue and swallowed any drops that landed on it. She lowered herself onto his face and he wrapped his arms around her legs to pull her down harder onto him. He lapped at the young pussy sat over him and ran his tongue between her folds. She tasted sweet and was sodden from her previous orgasm. He lapped at her nectar and delved his tongue inside her tight hole.

Violet had wrapped her fingers around his stiff cock and was rubbing her hand up and down his length. She placed her lips over the end of his cock and swirled her tongue around it. Her other hand was between her legs, inside her panties and she was rubbing her clit. She moaned a little around his cock and made small vibrations in her throat. This caused a muffled groan to come from him.

Jessica rubbed herself over his face and undid her top and bra to release her breasts. She took them in her hands and tweaked her nipples, making them hard. She massaged her pale globes and threw her head back as her pussy was eaten. His tongue was sliding in and out of her and she was loving it. He moved her forward a bit and slipped his tongue over her arsehole. He licked at her hole and made her squirm above him. He slipped back to her pussy and sucked on her clit, making her moan loudly.

Violet bobbed her head up and down on his cock and was rubbing her clit harder now. She shoved 2 fingers inside her own pussy and began pumping them into her. Her soft whimpers escaping through her mouth around the large cock still in there. Her panties were soaked as she made herself cum, her legs weakening beneath her and her body shuddering with the orgasm. She removed his cock from her mouth and sucked her fingers clean before returning to his cock.

Jessica felt the warmth of climax spread through her body and began to shake as he made her cum. Her juice flowed onto his tongue and he swallowed rapidly to get it all. His face was covered with her scent and he could not believe that he was being used by 2 young girls for sex. If anyone found out, his life would be ruined but at this moment he did not care. No-one was due to come to his office, so he had the time to enjoy himself. Jessica got off his face and told Violet to swap places. Violet stopped sucking his cock and moved round to sit on his face. She had turned the other way on his face. His nose was positioned on her clit and he dived his tongue into her pussy.

Jessica was not prepared to suck his cock; she climbed onto the table and straddled the headmaster. She parted her lips and placed his cock at her opening, before slowly sinking herself down onto his hard cock. She gritted her teeth as she was filled with his meat. She began to rock on his cock rubbing her clit on his pubic hair, it itched but it felt nice. She felt him grow more inside her, as her tight muscles clenched around him. She had planned on taking him slowly, she wanted to savour the moment that he became theirs and she had him literally eating out of their hands.

Violet was still dripping from her orgasm when she sat on his face, he lapped at her nectar and nuzzled her clit with his nose. Her aroma was more salty than sweet, and he wanted so much more of it. His tongue slid along her folds and occasionally slipped inside her. She gasped when he did, giving him the encouragement, he needed to continue. Her hands went to her breasts and she played with her tanned globes, she pinched her own nipples making them hard and sending little jolts of pleasure through her body. She felt her body tingle and warm as her next orgasm started. She could fell herself beginning to shake and she fidgeted on his face. He tried to hold her still, but she was strong and pulled away from him. Her body convulsed as her orgasm tore through her and she drenched his tongue in her juice. When she was done, she got off him and moved across the table to Jessica.

Jessica had increased the pace on his cock and was nearing her own climax. She watched Jessica move across the table towards her. She put her arm around Violet's neck and pulled her in for a kiss. Jessica slipped her tongue into Violet's mouth and swirled it around. Violet responded by entwining her tongue around Jessica's. He watched as the girls embraced each other and he found it a massive turn on. He wished he could be part of that too but focused on the girl riding his cock. Jessica was rocking harder now as she became engrossed in the kiss with her best friend. They had had plenty of practice as they would regularly fuck each other, during the nights when everyone else was asleep.

Master Williams was beginning to feel his own orgasm build, and he felt his balls twitch as he prepared to cum inside his pupil. He grasped her waist and pulled her down onto him harder. She could feel him beginning to spasm beneath her and she bobbed up and down on him. He grunted that he was cumming and he shot his load deep inside her. The feel of his hot cum inside her set off her own climax and she flooded his lap with her juice. As her climax subsided, she got off him and Violet immediately licked all her juice of his cock.

He watched as Violet cleaned him up and he began to get hard again. Violet stopped and told him to stand up. She also told Jessica to lay down on the desk. She bent over and wrapped her arms around her friend's legs and buried her face in her pussy. He took his cue and parted her cheeks to allow access to her pussy. He slipped his cock inside her and pumped into her. She wiggled her hips to get a better fit inside her and her groaned at how good that felt. She was eating Jessica and lapped at her folds. Jessica placed her hands on Violets head and pulled her into her harder. Violet sucked on Jessica's clit and nibbled it gently.

He watched as the girls played with each other, he loved seeing the contrast in the shape and skin colouring. Violet had a gorgeous plump ass which he was now fucking, Jessica had beautiful pale breasts with large nipples. Each had their own dominant feature. Jessica was obviously the leader with how well she had played him, but Violet knew what she wanted when it came to sex. He was not unhappy with the scenario, in fact it pleased him knowing that at any time they could come to him and demand attention. Attention that he was happy to give.

Violet could taste his cum in her friend's pussy. The sweet salty taste was amazing. She moved a hand and placed a finger inside Jessica's arse and wiggled it around. Jessica was moaning and Violet could feel her clench around her finger. She looked up to see Jessica staring back at her with her boobs in her hands. She held her gaze before Jessica flopped her head back and closed her eyes. Violet felt full of his cock inside her and she pushed back against his thrusts. With her other hand she put it between her legs and felt his balls slap against her legs. She held them and rubbed them gently, he groaned behind her and increased the pace of his thrusts. He gripped her waist as he pummelled into her. He slapped her across the backside, and she yelped into Jessica's pussy.

Jessica could feel Violets finger inside her butt, and she loved it. She rocked against her hand and could feel herself tingle all over. She wanted to cum for her and was getting close to doing so. She also wanted to taste her own juice and his seed, so she sat up and pulled Violet away from her pussy. As violet stood, Jessica kissed her hard on her mouth and Violet slipped her tongue between Jessica's lips. The taste of her own juice mixed with his cum was delightful. She was satisfied that she had tasted herself and lay back down to allow Violet to finish her off. He watched them kiss and wanted to taste it too, but he could wait, He moved his hands off Violet's hips and leant forward to grasp her breasts. Brushing his thumbs across her nipples, made her clench around him. He repeated the action and in turn it felt like she was sucking him with her vagina.

Violet wanted him to make her cum like he had Jessica. She pushed back harder and faster and she pumped her finger inside Jessica's ass. Jessica squeezed her muscles and felt the warmth flood through her, she gasped as her orgasm flowed and took hold of her, making her shudder and squirm at Violet's ministrations. Wave after wave of pleasure spread through Jessica's pussy and she flooded Violet's hand with her juice.

He could feel his nuts twitch and the heat flow through his body, he felt the fluid rise in his tubes, then spurt from the end of his dick. The hot jism hitting the inside of her caused her own climax to fire, her own body sending waves of spasms along her body and making her legs tremble beneath her. She collapsed forward onto Jessica, and he pulled out of her, withered but satisfied.

John and His Hot Step-Sisters: Family Business

John had come home from university after the passing of his father the day before. He was to assist his mother in the arrangements as he was now master of the house. His 2 stepsisters (1 from his father's first marriage, the other from his second) were already at the house. They had all grown up together in the big house, so they were all accustomed to where their rooms were. The girls had always dressed the same when they were growing up, but they led completely different lives now. Lorraine was into horses being a professional 3-day eventer and Samantha was a gothic artist. They had all shared a wing of the house and had spent many years running the halls and stairs playing hide and seek. John always had to find them first and they were always in the same spot together. When it was his turn to hide, they were cruel and left him to do something else. Despite this he loved them both. Maybe he loved them both a bit too much.

He had always had a bit of a thing for his big sisters. He would follow them like a lost sheep, wherever they would go. His room was in between the 2 of them and he had made small peep holes in the walls so he could watch them, at bedtime. He had in the past, stolen items of their clothing for keepsakes, claiming ignorance when they asked him about them. He had never done it so frequently as to cause real suspicion.

He went to see his mother in her chambers as she was devastated by the loss of her husband. He took her hand and kissed it. She was totally distraught. He hugged her tight and told her everything would be ok and that he would sort it all out. They chatted for a while and then he left her to rest. He was approaching his room when he saw his sisters on the stairs. They walked up and hugged him, asking him how he was and how their mother was coping. He told them that she was resting, and they could go see her later. He watched them walk away, heading towards Sam's room, and the familiar stirring started within his trousers. He hurried to his room, shutting the door behind him. He leant against it and closed his eyes. He waited for the sensation to pass, thinking of anything else but his sisters.

Once he had got control of his sense he went and laid on his bed. He thought about how he would miss his father and all the arrangements he had to make. He cried, feeling guilty about the lustful thoughts he had for his sisters. He knew it was wrong in normal circumstances, however at this time is was worse. The flow of emotions was overwhelming, and he sobbed to himself. He must have dosed off from the drain of emotions, but he could hear his sisters in the next room. They were laughing and giggling, and this piqued his interest. He went to the spy hole in his closet and looked through. He saw them on the bed together, they were having a pillow fight and there were feathers floating all over the room. At first, he thought that it was totally inappropriate, but he understood that they may only be trying to deal with the situation as best they could. Sam dived at Lorraine and tackled her. They landed in a heap on the covers and fell about laughing. Sam tried to pin Lorraine, but she got the better of Sam and pinned her instead. Sam lifted her head and licked the end of Lorraine's nose, making her cringe away. This started a licking battle and they tried to outdo each other. They both went in to lick each other at the same time and touched tongues. Sam stopped but Lorraine took advantage and kissed her.

John nearly cried out in surprise as they began kissing each other properly. Their hands wandering over the others body. Lorraine managed to place her hands either side of Sam's head. She held it whilst kissing her deeply. Their tongues now wrestling as they just were. Sam was now pulling at Lorraine's top, pulling it off over her head. She was wearing no bra and her pert little tits bobbed into view. Sam put her hand round one and pulled it into her mouth. She sucked and licked at the nipples making them hard and erect. John now had his hand down his trousers, firmly rubbing his cock.

Lorraine now unclothed Sam and returned the favour, she savoured Sam's breasts, appreciating the size of them. The girls were now just in their panties and Sam had straddled Lorraine's leg and was rubbing herself up and down it, trying to get the right friction on her clit. Her hand was inside Lorraine's pants playing with her clit. She pushed her fingers inside her and began pumping in and out of her. Lorraine flicked her tongue over Sam's nipples and kneaded her breasts. Sam pulled Lorraine from her boobs and returned to kissing her. Sam was pushing her fingers hard inside and rubbing her thumb on Lorraine's clitoris. Soft moans were coming from them both as they pleasured each other. John, still in his closet now had his hard cock out and was tugged on it with fervour. Seeing his sisters embracing in such a manner, made him feel better about himself. Suddenly the girls stopped and got off the bed. They moved out of sight which frustrated John immensely. He continued to think about what he had seen in order for him to bring himself off. He punished his cock with his hand as it flew along his shaft rapidly. Jism spurted out of the end of his cock just as the door to his closet flew open. The girls grabbed hold of him and pulled him into the room. Off balance, they pushed him back and into a chair. He was panicking that he had literally been caught with his trousers down, but they told him to stop fidgeting and it would all be over soon enough.

Between them, they lay the chair down on the floor, so he was facing the ceiling. They stood over him and told him that they knew what he had been doing all this time. They knew he had spied on them over the years and that he had had those wicked thoughts about them both. They told him that they had both put on shows for him, knowing that he was watching them. They also told him that they knew it was him stealing their clothes. They told him that he would now be punished for his lewd thoughts. Sam knelt on the floor with her knees either side of his head. She was facing his feet but looking him straight in the eye. She told him that they were going to do whatever they liked to him and he was not to make a sound. To make sure he stayed quiet, Lorraine removed her panties, bunched them up and placed them in his mouth. The smell of her sex wafted up his nose and he closed his eyes as the wave of euphoria washed over him. Sam watched as he did and laughed in his face. He felt a wave of shame briefly wash over him, but it was overpowered by the sense of lust.

She told him what a pathetic little man he was and that this was all for their gratification and he was just a means to an end. With that, she slipped off her own panties and pushed them into his mouth too. The mix of smells was intoxicating, and he felt his cock rising again. Sam shuffle forward and straddled him, she rubbed her cunt over his face. She used his nose as a clitoral stimulator. She moved back and forth on his nose, making him take in more of her scent. Meanwhile Lorraine had grabbed his cock with her slender fingers and was expertly wanking him off. She untied him from the chair and moved him of it. He lay prone on the floor as both sisters took advantage. She cupped his balls in her hand and gave them a hard squeeze. A moan escaped John's mouth, muffled by the fabric left in there, but still audible and he received a slap for his efforts. Lorraine leant forward and took his cock in her mouth. She slurped up and down on his dick taking in most of his long length, spittle flying everywhere at the speed of her head. She sunk her head right down on his cock that his entire cock was in her mouth. It twitched under her ministrations and he struggling to remain silent. Sam moved and took the panties out of John's mouth. She told him not to say anything but to just eat her and make her come. She then sat on his face again and waited or him to start licking. It was not long before his tongue lapped at her folds and clit. He reached up and wrapped his arms around her thighs to bring him down further onto his tongue. He shoved his tongue deep into her pussy. He immediately loved her taste.

Lorraine stopped sucking and moved up so she could sit on his cock. She parted her folds and sunk all the way down. She rocked back and forward getting the full use of the length. She was facing Sam as she rode his hard dick and she leant forward to kiss her. They continued to ride John whilst they played with each other's tits. They upped the pace of their movements in order to bring themselves off. As they both began to climax, their combined moans set off John's own orgasm. He felt the warmth spread from his balls and the fluid rising in his cock. He came hard inside Lorraine as she flooded his lap with her cum. Sam felt her body tingle as the sensations built within her. She felt her pussy clench a few times and her body shuddered as came on John's tongue, covering his face with her nectar.

They swapped places. Sam now playing with his cock and balls trying to make him hard again. It did not take long before she felt him swell in her hands and watched as his cock grew. She planted soft kisses along its length, tasting Lorraine's cum on it as well as his.

Lorraine sat the opposite way to Sam and planted her pussy onto his face. He stuck out his tongue and tasted his own seed mixed with her glorious scent. He lapped at the liquid seeping from her hole and swallowed as much as he could. She rubbed herself all over his face and he licked everywhere that touched his tongue. She shuffled forward slightly, and her knotted hole was above his mouth. He licked at it hearing the squelching sound that it made. Her smell was overwhelming, and he wanted to taste it forever. He knew that this was to be his only chance to have them both, and he was determined to make the most of it. Despite the girls thinking they were in charge he was happy to take their orders as he had dreamt of this moment for an awfully long time.

Sam lowered herself onto his hard cock and began to bounce up and down on it. She was surprised to find how much he filled her. She was also surprised to find out how much she enjoyed toying with him. Lorraine and her, had been meeting up for a while to discuss this scenario and they had always ended up in bed together. He must have thought that this was a first for them, but they had been sleeping together or years.

Lorraine was playing with her own boobs to assist in her orgasm. She was rocking herself against his face to get more friction on her clit as he sucked at her arsehole. She could feel the warm tingling sensation begin to flow through her body and she let it build, she wanted her climax to be big and it was getting bigger by the second. She felt her pussy twinge and then flood as her orgasm washed over her. She groaned into the air as she came over his face and he lapped at her juice as it leaked out of her.

He felt the warm liquid flow over his face, and he drink from her hole. This excited him more and he could feel his balls tighten. The sensation of his orgasm flowing through him was amazing, he tingled all over and felt the fluid flow up his cock and spurt out of his dick.

Sam felt him cum inside her, the hot liquid jetted into her pussy and fill her with his seed. That feeling set off her own orgasm and own juice flooded her womb and seeped out of her. She groaned as she came and juddered on his body.

She pushed herself up off him and helped Lorraine up as well. They left him splayed on the floor covered in juice and cum. His smile on his face told them that he had enjoyed it as much as they had. Sam took Lorraine's hand and led her out of the room. John rolled onto his side and curled up into the recovery position. He picked up their panties and held them to his nose. He took a deep breath and savoured the scent of them both. He felt amazing. He had dreamed of this day for years, never believing it would happen. He was happy and contented and he had been left with keepsakes, so he could relive the memories with added smells.

Betrayal and the Sexy Revenge

Paul and Karen had been together for 3 years. They had been married for 2. They were both flirty people and loved to play games with each other, seeing who could pull on a night out. They had never slept with anyone else, but it was always fun. Paul was half Italian and had the light tanned skin permanently. Karen was a gorgeous brunette with a big smile and a well-proportioned body. They had a wide circle of friends and an active social life. Weekends were a fulltime party and even nights during the week could see them out at karaoke bars, wine tastings, and anything else they fancied doing.

They were the "It" couple of their social group and were also the marriage guidance for the group. Everyone in the area knew who they were. The neighbours never complained about the loud music as they were all in attendance to the parties. They were always together, apart from when they were at work. Paul was a construction supervisor and earnt a lot of money, Karen owner her own cosmetic business which was the most successful one in the city.

One day whilst at work, Paul was on a business lunch with a client. They had sat outside the busy restaurant which was busy and as it was a beautiful day they did not mind. He was talking to the client when he saw his wife walk past and go into a restaurant opposite. He could see through the windows and saw her walk to a table where their neighbour sat. He stood to meet her and leant forward. Paul assumed he would kiss her cheek, but he gave her a full-on wet kiss which was reciprocated. Paul was fuming. He had told Karen that he was meeting a client today but had not decided on where to take them. Luckily for Paul the meal with his client was nearing its end and he had cleared his schedule for the rest of his day. He had planned on going to the salon to take Karen home and cook her dinner.

Paul managed to take control of his attention and bring it back to the task at hand, but occasionally took a quick glance over there. The meeting went well, and the client had signed a new agreement for more than a thousand new buildings on the outskirts of the city. He thanked the client for coming and when they left, he sat back down and ordered a drink. He watched as his wife and neighbour ate a small lunch then got up to leave. He waited for them to exit the restaurant and he intended on following them. He got up having paid for the meal and walked in the direction they had gone. He followed them for a few blocks, and he watched them head into a hotel. This would only mean one thing.

He decided to go home and make a few calls. When he got back, he called the salon. He asked where she was and was told that she had gone home for the day as she had got a bad headache. He accepted the explanation and then called his neighbour. When Sophie answered, He asked to speak to Kevin, and was told that Kevin was away on business and would not be back until the following day. He told her that he would call round tomorrow to speak to him.

Paul sat there stewing over the situation. His phone beeped, he picked it up to find a message from Karen. "Sorry to drop this on you but we have had a spot inspection from the Inland Revenue, and I will be here late tonight. Pleased don't wait up xxx". He threw his phone across the room and it shattered into tiny pieces.

An idea popped into his head and he thought seriously about it. He called Sophie back, when she answered, he told her that Karen had to work late, and as they were both alone, would she like to come over and he would make them dinner. She replied that she would love to, and she told him she would be over in an hour.

Paul went to the kitchen and threw together and quick and easy meal and then went to the cellar to get a few bottles of good wine out. He laid the table and prepared the room for her to come over. He then went to get changed and to make the bed. He sprayed himself with his nicest aftershave and tidied himself up.

The doorbell rang an hour later, and he opened it to let Sophie in. She stood there in a pretty, floral dress that clung to her in the right places. She was a curvy woman and he was happy that she was with him. He followed her through to the kitchen and pulled her chair out for her. She sat down and he dished up the dinner. She said it looked lovely and she began to eat the pasta dish. She told him how delicious it was. He poured her a glass of wine and one for himself. They chatted about work and the current political state, making small talk whilst they ate. She drank the wine quickly and he poured her another. It was a sweet wine but was strong. She began to giggle as the alcohol took effect.

He told her that he needed to tell her something and that she was not going to like shat she heard. He told her what he had seen this afternoon and that he had followed them both to the hotel, that he had called her salon to be told she had gone home early due to a headache, and that he had received a message telling him she was working late. He let the information sink in, and she became upset. He went to her and held her as she broke down. She asked how they could do it to them and he could not answer. Tears ran down her cheeks and he wiped them away with his fingers. He showed her compassion and she responded likewise. She took his feelings into account and she held him tight.

They stood in the kitchen, just holding each other tight. He kissed her on the head as he tried to calm her down and she lifted her head to look at him. Confusion spread across her face as she tiptoed up and softy kissed his lips. He pulled back and she apologised. She went to push him away, but he pulled her into him again. It was his turn to kiss her and it was soft and gentle. They parted their lips and their tongues explored their mouths. She slid her hand up his shoulder and into the hair at the back of his head. She grasped it gently, pulling him into the kiss. He kissed her harder now and with more passion and she moaned softly into his mouth. He bent and picked her up, then sat her on the table. He pushed everything off and onto the floor, plates and glasses smashing everywhere. They ignored it and continued kissing. She wrapped her legs around his waist as they embraced.

She began undoing her buttons on the front of her dress, but he slid his hands up her thighs and grasped her bum. She pulled him into her and rubbed her crotch against his. He was hard and wanted her. She ripped at his clothes removing his shirt and running her hands over his chest. His hands were on her shoulders now pulling her into him as his kisses got deeper. He lifted her dress up over her head and returned his tongue to her mouth. She was not wearing a bra and he lowered her back, so she lay on the table. He planted kisses down her body, over her collar bone and onto her chest. He took a breast in each and pushed them together so he could lick both nipples at the same time. She gasped as he did, her body aching for him to be inside her. He massaged her pale boobs as he licked and sucked on her nipples.

He removed his trousers and she gasped at how big he was. And slipped her small hands around the shaft. She began to rub his cock as he kissed her again and he moaned into her mouth. She begged him to fuck her now and he could not resist.

He parted her legs and moved in between them, he opened up her sex and slid his cock inside her. She inhaled deeply and let it out slowly as she accustomed herself to his girth. He slowly began to move inside her, and she moaned at how good it felt. He gradually increased how far he pulled out before entering her again. She was getting used to his size and she rocked back on his cock as he pushed into her. She had not felt this excited since she married Kevin and their sex life had become stale. She grabbed the edge of the table as he pressed against her and she wanted to scream. Her gasps coming in noisy ragged bursts.

She could feel every inch on him inside her and it was a wonderful sensation. Compared to her husband, he was huge, and she thought he was going to split her in half. She parted her legs further so he could get more of himself inside her. He increased the pace and began to fuck her harder, she groaned loudly and was pushing herself back onto him. She looked at him and told him she needed him deeper. He pulled out of her and pulled her off the table. He spun her round and bent her over the table. She parted her legs and he entered her again. This time she howled as he hit her g-spot, she growled at him to fuck her harder and he grabbed her hips and pummelled her. The sound of his balls slapping her thighs was regular and she growled with each thrust. She twisted slightly and placed her arm over her back and played with her bum hole. She dipped her finger into it at the same time as he thrust into her. She felt her body warm as the start of her orgasm washed over her.

She gripped him tight as he pumped his cock into her pussy. His balls tightened and he grunted as his semen fired out of his dick. The hot jism pumping against her insides, made her body shudder as her own cum mixed with his. She screamed as her climax ripped through her and she collapsed on the table.

He pulled out of her as his cock became flaccid. She sat up on the table breathing hard. She had not come like that for years and she was not ready to stop now. She jumped down off the table and dropped to her knees. She began sucking her own juice off his cock and playing with his balls to make him hard again. She needed more of his cock. He picked her up and carried her up the stairs. She sat on his marital bed and slid her mouth around the head of his penis again. She took as much of his as her mouth would allow, and she held him there while she sucked on him. He placed his hand on her head and she began bobbing on it. He could feel himself getting harder as she tended to his cock and there was much that he wanted to do to her.

He pulled out of her mouth and gently pushed her back on the bed. He lowered himself and gently blew on her clit, she shivered, not from cold but from pleasure and he planted kisses around her pussy. She smiled at the attention he was giving her and when he slipped a couple of fingers inside her, she grabbed the bed covers and arched her back. He gripped her hips and held her to the bed. He was strong and she loved the idea of him pinning her and taking control over her body. He sucked on her clit hard and she clamped her legs against his head. He pried them apart again and slid a finger into her bum. She screamed with delight as she rocked on his hands. She wanted to feel him in her arse properly and she was sure he would do it at some point. Her body ached from the energy already expelled and the sensations rippling through her.

He rammed his fingers into both her holes, and he watched as fluid seeped from her pussy. He smiled knowing that he was satisfying her so much. He could feel her muscles tightening around her fingers and how they contracted around them. He pushed harder and she screams as her orgasm ripped through her. His hands were covered in sticky juice and he smiled. She lay there for a few minutes getting her breath back and he joined her on the bed. He bent down and planted light kisses all over her face. She shifted her position and straddled him. She lifted herself slightly and took hold of his cock. She rubbed the head of his penis against her clit and then she slowly lowered herself onto his pole. She gasped again as she took him inside her, and he groaned as he felt her tight pussy slide down his shaft. He held her hips while she adjusted her position to get comfortable. She then began to slowly rise up and down on his length. She grabbed her own breasts and began tugging on her own nipples. Her head was back as she rode his cock. Her slim body working itself towards another climax. He watched as her muscles worked in her core and her legs. He found that she enjoyed his body more than his wife did recently but then he knew why. He closed his eyes and imagined Karen walking in on them now, he smiled at the idea but thought it was not going to happen. He focused on Sophie again and how she was working his cock.

He let her set the pace and he was happy with it. At this speed he would not cum for a while, but she probably would. As she lowered herself onto him, he started to push up, only subtly but enough to make a difference. She was groaning at him and she looked him in the eye. She wanted him to see her face as she came but she was not there yet. Her body had become accustomed to his size now and she increased her pace. Her boobs bounced as she rode him. He lifted his hands to steady them and he gently pinched her nipples. She growled at him and she asked him to help her. He put his hands back on her hips and pulled her down and thrust up into her.

He pounded into her pussy and she placed her hands on his chest as she rocked on him faster. He flipped her over, so she was on her back and he grabbed her legs and put them over his shoulders. The angle that his cock now hit was deeper than he had ever been. She clung onto the bed sheets as he thrust deeper into her. She cried out as his cock hit her g-spot hard. The headboard banged against the wall as his pace fastened. He pumped his cock into her, wanting her to cum again and again on his cock. She squeezed her legs around his head as another climax hit and she gushed out around his cock. He grunted hard as he filled her with cum, his balls clenching to release all of his semen. He slid out of her and rolled onto his back. He was hot and sweaty and so was she. A sheen of sweat covered her body and she glistened in the light.

She looked over at him and smiled. Her breathing now back to normal. She turned her back on him and dragged his arm over her, so they were spooning. She wriggled her bum against his groin and could feel his reaction. He asked her if she was a nymphomaniac, and she replied that she just enjoyed good sex. She also commented that she liked anal if he was up to it.

He laughed and asked if that was a challenge. She replied that it was.

He rubbed his groin back against her arse and she pushed back against him. She was still slippery from the previous session and lifted her leg to allow access. He slipped a finger between her legs and scooped some liquid and rubbed it around her puckered hole. He slipped his finger inside her and began circling around. He wanted to make sure she was relaxed before he entered her. He did not want to hurt her. He felt her relax around his finger, so he added another. He buttocks clenched as he did, and he held his hand still until she relaxed again. Once she did, he pulled out his fingers and slid his cock inside. He stayed still for a few seconds then began to rock back and forward slowly. He could feel how restrictive her rectum was around him and he gradually began to increase the speed.

She inhaled through gritted teeth and let out a long "Yesssssssssssssss". Her hand went between her own legs as she fingered herself. She was sopping wet from him fucking her in so many different ways. She wandered if this would be just a one off? She hoped it was not as she could really use a man like this in her life. Keven never gave her anal sex, he said it was too dirty. The climax she got from this position was euphoric and he denied her that pleasure. She was unsure if she would ever take Kevin back, especially with a man like Paul living next door.

Her ass was full of cock and she was in heaven. She had not been done in the back passage for years and if felt just as good as it did the first time. She did not want Paul to ever stop fucking her. She purred her contentment and he was increasing his speed in her ass. She did not growl at him this time, she kept holding her breath not wanting it to be over. He ploughed into her ass harder now and she could hear his body slapping against hers. She could feel the sweat building on him as it did on her. She bent forward slightly and opened herself up more. He pulled onto her hips as he penetrated her. Her body clamped against his, it was shivering as her body coped with the mass in her rear. She turned her head and looked him in the eyes. "Do it" she said, "make me cum again, I'm ready". He pushed into her as far as he would go then pulled all the way out. She groaned as he left her body and he slammed into her hard. "Arghhhhhhh" was all that came from her as she was filled again. He continued to pull right out and then shove back in again and she wanted him to do it harder. As he pushed in, she pushed back, and she convulsed around his cock. He did not stop despite her climax and she carried on cumming. He heard the bedroom door open as he continued to bring her off and he saw Karen stood there with her mouth open.

The anger on her face was a picture and Paul just smiled at her. Sophie now saw her stood there, but just closed her eyes again as she let Paul carry on. Karen was yelling about how she was disgusted by the scene and how dare he cheat on her. He ignored her outrage until Sophie had finished then he pulled out and lay back on the bed. Sophie turned and rest her arm across his body.

Karen asked what he had to say for himself. He replied, "Hello Karen how is your headache?" She looked confused and asked what he meant. "When I called your office today, I was told you had left early as you had a bad headache" Then I saw you and Kevin head into a hotel after seeing you kiss each other in the restaurant. I then spoke to Sophie to ask where Kevin was, and she told me he was away on business and would not be back until tomorrow. I then get a message from you telling me that you had a surprise inspection and wouldn't be home until late."

"What would you make of all that information Karen?" He asked. She Started to say something and then stopped.

"I asked Sophie over to tell her what I had discovered, and we were consoling each other for your betrayal, and we decided that if you two could go off and fuck each other, then so could we!"

"I feel this is fair, Sophie thinks it is fair, what about you?"

Karen turned on her heels and went to the spare room, she grabbed a case and came back into the bedroom. She emptied her drawers and wardrobes and slammed them shut. She picked up the case and stormed out.

"I guess we know the answer then?" He said to Sophie, who giggled beside him.

Lydia and her first Party with a bang!

Lydia Had just turned 18 and her friend Jack was taking her out somewhere special. She had no idea where nor what they would do when they got there but Jack said she would enjoy herself. She trusted him completely having been friends with him since she was 5. He was a year older than her and he had way more experience in life that she had. Her parents had been extremely strict with her as she grew up, but they had died recently, and Jack also wanted to cheer her up.

Jack drove them to a house in the country and she had no idea who's house it was. He helped her out of the car and lead her to the house. He opened the door and the room in front of her were filled with her friends. They had thrown her a surprise party and she was ecstatic. She had never had a party, nor had she drunk alcohol or smoked. She was ready to put all of that behind her and have fun for the first time in her life.

The party started with loud music and plenty of beer. She was given her first glass and she knocked it back. She drank half the glass in one go and let out a loud belch. Everyone laughed and she went round to thank everyone for coming. Whenever her glass was empty a full was put in its place. She was gradually getting drunk and she got the giggles. She danced, and smoked the night away until the early hours, when people started leaving. She said goodbye to them all as they searched for her to say thank you for the evening.

When most of the guests had left, she found Jack sat on the sofa with a few of her friends. She grabbed his hands and pulled him up to dance with him. He reluctantly joined her, and she danced like a drunk person whilst the upbeat tunes were playing. When the slower songs were played, she got close to him and ground herself against him. He was surprised at how well she moved, considering her parents had not allowed any music of hers in the house. They only listened to classical or to Sir Cliff Richards as that was wholesome music.

Lydia performed the perfect slut drop and received a round of applause for her efforts. Jack was gobsmacked that she knew how to do that too. She was full of surprises. He had assumed that by this late in the night, she would be passed out of the sofa already. Sweat was covering her body as she danced, and she removed the shirt she had on over her string strap top. Her pert breasts jiggled as she danced, and they were attracting a lot of attention, including a lot from Jack. She turned her back on him and backed up to him as she wiggled her butt. The reaction he had in his groin, was not unlike any other guy in the room watching her.

She flung her arm around his neck and swayed in front of him. She ground herself against his crotch then turned to face him and she lifted a leg and wrapped it around his waist, he placed a hand on her bottom as she did and he bent forward and kissed her forehead. She stopped and looked at him before pulling him down into a passionate embrace. She swirled her tongue around his mouth before pulling away and dancing in front of one of her other friends. He inhaled deeply and blew it out slowly. He had not though of her in that manner before, but she had stirred something within him now and was not to be sated until he had her.

She was now dancing with Jodie and she was grinding against her too. Jodie had that look in her eyes that Jack recognised. If Lydia were not careful, Jodie would try it on with her and he was not sure that Lydia was ready for that. He was the only one in the room that knew she was a virgin, and as she had never been in this situation before, she could herself into some trouble.

Lydia seemed to know what she was doing when she began to fondle Jodie's breasts through her top. She then pulled Jodie in for a deep kiss. Everyone watched as the girls kissed and a few wolf whistles were heard along with a few cheers. Jodie and Lydia didn't seem to hear them as they began removing each other clothes. More cheers erupted and whoop was let out by someone else. Jack stood in the corner watching with interest. Jodie was now bare chested, and Lydia was playing with her firm, round tits. She watched as Jodie's nipples reacted to stimulation and hardened. Jodie was happy to let her carry on exploring her body. Lydia planted kisses all over her body. Starting from her neck and working down. She kissed all along her collar bone, using tiny little nibbles along it too and wrapped her arms around Lydia's head and pulled her in tight. She was enjoying the exploration of her body. Lydia ran her hand down her torso to the elasticated waist of her shorts and ran her thumbs along the inside of the material. She looked Jodie in the eye before kissing her and gently biting her lip. She pulled down Jodie's shorts and dropped them to the floor. Jodie stepped out of them and flicked them across the room to the sofa. Her pink lace panties were the only thing she had left on and Lydia stepped back to admire the beautiful sight before her.

Jodie's skin was tanned and toned. She was not overly muscular more athletic. She stood with her hands on her hips, and one leg bent and off to the side. Her brown hair falling down to her shoulders. She obviously sunbathed topless as her breasts were tanned and her nipples dark. Lydia pointed at her then beckoned her over with one finger. When Jodie reached her, she put her arms around her neck and kissed her again. Jodie's hands wrapped around her waist before placing a thumb in the top of Lydia's skirt, which was tartan, including the wrap around part and buckle holding it together. Jodie undid the buckle and let the material drop to the floor. Lydia was now in her vest top and panties. Her light pink top matched Jodie's underwear and Jodie pushed her hands up under it and slipped it off over her head.

Lydia was pale in comparison to Jodie, her breasts smaller but her hips were wider, and she carried a little more weight. Both were stunning in their own way and seeing them together made Jack and the other men horny. Jodie's hand went up to Lydia's pale orbs and she groped them, running her thumbs across her nipples, making Lydia gasp. Jodie smiled and kissed her breasts in circular motions. Slowly moving closer to the nipple as she went. When she got to it, she opened her mouth and enveloped the stiff bud, using her tongue to flick it. She moved from one to the other, doing the same thing. Lydia's breathing had changed to short gasps as she became turned on by the woman before her.

Jack could not believe that Lydia's first sexual experience would be with a woman. Jodie took the lead and manoeuvred Lydia to the sofa where she made her sit down. She hooked her arms under Lydia's legs, and she pulled her to the edge of the sofa. Jodie knelt on the floor and put her hands on Lydia's thighs and pushed them apart. She lowered her head and nuzzled at her crotch. She pulled the wet material to one side and licked Lydia's clit. Her tongue flicked the little bud and then slide between the folds of her sex before delving inside her. Lydia gasped as Jodie licked her pussy. She had only ever touched herself down there and she would never have dreamed that she would be in this position. Her parents would be turning in their graves if they could see her now. She watched as Jodie pushed her tongue inside her and she felt amazing. She never knew sex could be like this. She relaxed and allowed Jodie to pleasure her. She felt that tingle start somewhere deep down and let it wash over her. He shook as her climax ran through her and she felt Jodie lapping furiously at the nectar pooling in her pussy.

Jodie pulled her mouth away from Lydia's pussy and it glistened in the light as it was slick with her juice. Jodie looked directly at Lydia as she pushed 2 fingers easily inside her. This feeling was not unusual to Lydia as she had done this to herself when she was in bed. Laying there in the moonlight, exploring her own body while her parents slept in the next room. She was not used to making any noise when her body reacted to her touch, as she had not wanted to let them know what she was doing. Here though, she did not care. She allowed herself to make as much noise as she wanted. Her guttural growls indicating her enjoyment.

As Jodie pumped her fingers into Lydia, Lydia played with her boobs, rubbing her nipples, and tugging on them to get her there faster. She felt her womb warm as the blood flowed to it in response to the stimulation. She could feel the tingles starting again and she could hear her heart beating in her ears. Waves of pleasure washed over her as she came again, and she drenched Jodie's hand in her cum.

When her body had recovered from 2 orgasms in such a short space of time, she looked around the room to see that most of the men either had their dicks out or were stroking them through the material of their trousers. Jack in particular was stood there with cock in hand staring at the girls with lust in his eyes. She had never seen him look at her like that and she beckoned him over. He sat next to her on the sofa and lowered his head to her breast. He cupped the milky orb in his hand before taking her nipple into his mouth and swirling it around. She felt a twinge in her pussy, and she smiled at the feeling. He looked up at her and she smiled down at him, she whispered to him that she wanted him to be the first man to penetrate her as she trusted him not to hurt her. He nodded his accent and she indicated that she was ready.

Jack positioned himself between her legs and rubbed his cock at the entrance to her pussy. She was still slick with her juice and it slid along her folds easily. He looked up at her again to make sure she was still happy for him to go ahead and she nodded. He gently nudged her, and he watched as her hole stretched to allow him to enter her. It had been a while since he had taken someone virginity and he was happy she had chosen him to take hers. He took it slowly as he entered her, allowing her to adjust to his girth and length, and when she was ready, she gave him the nod to enter her fully. He slid inside her and she felt incredibly tight around him. She cried out as her hymen broke and he stopped. He did not move for a moment until she told him to continue. She gently pulled back, almost to the point where he slipped out of her, then slowly pushed back into her. She sucked the air in through gritted teeth but urged him to carry on. He moved a bit faster now and she moaned softly to him. He was being cautious as he really did not want to hurt her. He continued slowly until she wrapped her arms around him, placed her hands on his butt and pulled him into her.

He asked her if she were ok, and that he could carry on properly. She told him she was fine and wanted the full experience. He grasped her hips and pulled her onto him. His cock hit the top of her cervix and she groaned. He plunged into her faster now and she began to cry out, he did not break his stride as he recognised the type of cry. His cock was buried deep inside and she was pushing back against him. He moved his hands and grabbed her legs, lifting them and placing them over his shoulders. This change the angle of penetration and she grabbed hold of the sofa covering, pulling against it.

She was now screaming as he drove his shaft into her. He watched as her breasts swayed with each thrust and he took hold of one and squeezed it hard. She growled at him as she was overcome by her orgasm and he felt her tighten up around him, making his balls twitch and contract. He felt his cum rising from his sack and he shot his hot liquid into her. Her tight pussy milked his cum from his cock and she cried out with the waves washing through her. When he was empty and she had relaxed around him, he held her. She looked at him and mouthed the words "thank you". He pulled out of her and was surprised to see a queue of people behind him. He looked back at her worried that she would be scared by what was before her, but something flashed in her eyes and he knew she would be ok.

Jack sat down next to Jodie, who rested her head on his shoulder. She whispered to him how amazing that girl was. Jack replied that she had been a virgin up until this night and Jodie sat up and looked at him. She asked if he meant girl on girl virgin, he replied no virgin, virgin.

Steve had waited patiently for Jack to finish fucking Lydia and when she looked at him with hunger in her eyes he stepped forward. She reached up and pulled him down so she could kiss him, she grabbed him by the back of the neck as she swirled her tongue around his mouth and gently bit his bottom lip. He placed his hand between her legs and rubbed her mound while they kissed. She bucked her hips to meet his hand and groaned into his mouth. He pulled back from the kiss and pulled her up from the sofa, he turned her round and made her kneel on it before bending and licking her pussy from behind. His nose sat on her arsehole and she fell a weird sensation as is it pushed at her starfish. He licked up and swirled his tongue around it before standing up again. She shuffled in behind her and opened her lips to plunge his thick cock inside her.

She gasped as her pussy was stretched to fit around him and he remained still for a moment to allow her to relax. As soon as she had, he pushed into her and she nearly toppled over with the amount of force he used. She put her hands on the back of the sofa and straightened them so she could push back against him and to keep her balance. He placed his hand on her back and with the other one pushed a finger into her virgin ass. She lunged forward as his finger slipped inside and once she had become accustomed to it she pushed back again, and he increased the pace. She was groaning loudly as he ploughed into her and she threw her head back. Her eyes were closed and her mouth wide open as she reached another climax on his cock. He continued to push through it sending wave after wave of pleasure through her. She came a few times before his balls clenched and he unloaded his seed into her. He grunted as he came then slowed down as his balls emptied. He moved away from her and she slumped on the sofa.

Steve went and sat next to Jack and Jodie. He was surprised that she was still going with the amount of alcohol she had consumed.

Lydia looked up and saw Mike stood there with his cock in his hand, she shuffled to the edge of the seat and took hold of the dick bobbing in front on of her. She moved her hand slowly up and down as she looked up at Mike and opened her mouth. She covered the head and slowly bobbed her head down his shaft, she took as much as she could before drawing back up it. She pulled it out of her mouth and swirled her tongue around the head. He moaned as she slipped her mouth back over him, and she fondled his balls as she did. She had a hand between her legs flicking her bean and dipping her fingers inside herself. She saw George sit on the sofa next to her as she sucked on Mike's cock.

George picked her up and put her on his lap. He opened her lips and slid his rod inside her. She rocked back on his length and adjusted her positioning to tie in with the motion of her sucking Mike. She rode George's cock and sucked on Mikes dick, she had never felt anything like this, she was amazed that so many people wanted to fuck her and appreciated whet she was doing. It did not occur to her that she was being used as a piece of meat, she was just having fun with her friends and having great sex at the same time. Her thoughts returned to the situation at hand and she slurped on Mike's long shaft. George was holding her hips as she bounced on his cock. She still had a hand between her legs and rubbing her clit hard. She loved the feel of having 2 holes filled at the same time, and she imagined having her ass filled too. She wondered if that would happen tonight, and she thought it was entirely possible.

She could hear the squelches of her pussy and her mouth, and she felt euphoric. She wished this had happened before tonight, but it was such a special occasion. She felt Mike's balls tighten and she prepared herself for the rush of fluid to fill her mouth. George was pulling her down onto his crotch and she tensed up around him. She heard the boys groan together as they ejaculated inside her. She swallowed Mike's seed as he unloaded into her mouth and the hot seed pumping into her pussy, made her cum too. She was getting tired physically, but her mind was stimulated by the scenario. She loved the fact that she had a queue for her attention.

She looked over to see the group now sat together on the other sofa. 5 people that she had had some sort of sexual connection. She felt bad that she had not returned the favour to Jodie. She stood up and walked on weakened legs to the sofa and knelt on the floor. She stroked Jodie's legs and made her way up her thighs to her groin. Jodie smiled down at Lydia and opened her legs wide. Lydia leant forward and placed her mouth over Jodie's clit. She licked it gently at first then began to suck on it harder. She ran her tongue all over her and then dipped her tongue inside to taste her for the first time. She was sweet with a twang of salty mixed in. Lydia was hooked and she lapped at the nectar. She felt someone behind her part her own lips and shove their cocks into her. She did not care who is was now she just wanted more. She looked up and saw Jodie with someone's cock in her mouth. The sight of her sucking on a cock made her feel jealous and turned on at the same time. She wanted Jodie for herself but loved the fact that everyone was getting involved.

Someone came to the side of Jodie and she grabbed his cock too. The girls were surrounded by men all vying for gratification. Another cock was pushed on front of Lydia and she stopped eating Jodie and took the cock into her mouth. She pushed a couple of fingers inside Jodie instead, and pumped them into her. The man attached to the cock that Lydia had in her mouth began fucking her face. He held the back of her head and pushed it onto his cock. She gagged briefly as it hit the back of her throat and she relaxed her throat and allowed him to thrust into her further. She felt the cock in her pussy throb as it shot its hot semen inside her, they withdrew and were immediately replaced by someone else.

Jodie groaned as Lydia's fingers strummed inside her and she came hard on her fingers. She soaked Lydia's hand with her juice and instead of taking her fingers away, she added another one. She also sucked hared on the cock in her mouth which was soon taken away and her face was covered as he shot his load over her. He moved away and another cock took its place. She had no idea who was fucking her or who she was sucking but she felt incredible. She came on the cock inside her and as she gripped him with her pussy muscles he pulled out and came on her arse.

The next man to approach spat on her and rubbed it into her bum hole. He slid his cock slowly into her arse and she stopped everything else to adjust to the tight feeling in her rectum. When she relaxed her began to thrust into her, gently at first then increased the pace. She continued to play with Jodie's pussy and suck on the cock that was in her mouth. Her tiredness had gone, her body was tingling with the mixtures of sensations, she was horny and euphoric. Her body trembled with the exertion of holding herself up and rom the amount of people she had been with. Her pussy felt sore and bruised and she could feel cum dripping out around the cock that was in her. Her nipples had been pulled on, pinched, tweaked and sucked and they would probably take days to go back to normal. Her knees hurt where she had been on them so long, but she rocked back against the man that was fucking her. The cock in her mouth bobbed and exploded in her and she swallowed that too. When it pulled out, she expected another cock to replace it, but none came. She looked around the room and there were bodies laying everywhere. Most of the men were spent. Those that were still going were close to cuming. Jodie was breathing hard as she climaxed again on Lydia's fingers. She removed them and licked them clean. The guy with his dick in Jodie's mouth thrust faster and pulled out to shoot his jism over her tits. Just as he did this the guy, she was playing with erupted onto her chest too and it dripped off her nipples. The men collapsed on the sofa beside her and she flopped down further onto the couch herself.

As Lydia looked around again the only person, she could not see was Jack, she turned her head and looked back over her shoulder as he pulled out and pumped his cum on her ass. Her arse was sore from him fucking it, but she felt awesome. She was so happy and content, that this was the best birthday ever. She was glad that she had not had sex before tonight and she could not wait to talk about it with Jack later. She stood to try and find her clothes. As she did gravity took hold and the cum dribbled down her legs. She smiled to herself and picked up her underwear. She could not remember her panties coming off, but she did not care.

She still did not know whose house this was, but she would help clean it up when she had had some sleep. She went upstairs to the bathroom and looked at herself in the mirror. Her makeup was ruined, her hair was a mess, but her face was glowing. She cleaned herself up and got dressed. She went into a bedroom and lay on the bed. It was not long before she fell asleep.

Sub Zero

I was feeling kind of low and stressed, due to the pressures if work. I worked in insurance and the job was extremely high demand. As a thirty something woman, with her own house and car, mortgage that I was paying a small fortune for, I had been working as many hours as possible and it was taking its toll. It was the weekend and I had invited my best friend Rory round for a movie and pizza. I had my comfort pj's on and was waiting for him to turn up. We had been friends since college and spent as much time together as possible, but due to his new job, we had not seen each other for months. Everything was ready for when he arrived, the pizza had been cut, the wine poured, the corn had been popped and the movie paused at the beginning.

He had told me earlier that week that he had something to tell me, and I was eager to find out what. Rory was always getting into mischief of all forms, so I assumed it was something he had done whilst he was away. I was so excited about seeing him tonight and I was getting impatient for his arrival. I was sat on the sofa, clock watching waiting to hear the door go. I did not wait long before I heard it open and a cheery "hello" bounce its way up the corridor. I leapt up from my seat and ran to meet him. We flung our arms around each other and kissed cheeks. He removed his coat as I dragged him to the living room, where we flopped on the sofa together. I was so pleased to see him, that I started blurting out everything that had gone on with me since we had last seen each other. I explained that work was hectic, that I had been out a few times to our favourite haunt and that the regulars had kept me busy. He sat patiently listening to all I had to tell him, and laughed when I had told him that I had dropped a bottle of hot sauce on the floor in the kitchen, and It took me 3 days to get rid of the smell and the stains had not come out of the clothes I was wearing that day.

We laughed, giggled, cried, and talked for about an hour before he finally interrupted me and reminded me that he needed to tell me something. I stopped talking and waited for him to start. He was looking at his hands, which he was wringing together. I could tell he was nervous about telling me, so I placed my hand on his leg to urge him on and he flinched. He stood up and apologised for flinching. My look showed the concern I was feeling, I did not want my best friend feeling hurt by me. I stayed sitting but assured him that whatever he needed to say, could not be that bad and that he should not feel nervous discussing it with me. He sat back down and began his story. He told me that whilst he was away, he had gone to a club. A club that was for a certain type of person. He must have noted the confusion in my expression as he carried on explaining that it was a fetish club. My surprise must have been obvious as he stopped talking again. We had known each other for years and this was the first mention of anything like this. He continued to describe the club, with the individual booths for exhibitionist/voyeuristic play. The rooms for private play. That people walked round with masks on being led by others carrying whips etc. He elaborated that there were cages hanging with "slaves" inside that were to be totally ignored, as that was their punishment. It sounded so surreal. It sounded so exciting and I wished that I had been there with him.

I asked him how he felt about going and he told me that he enjoyed the experience, but that it had stirred something within him that he had not felt before. I asked him to explain and he told me that he had sometimes wondered what it would be like to be dominated but did not have the confidence to try anything. He also stated that he knew I was incredibly open minded and that I would not feel differently about him. I smiled and told him everything would be ok and gave him a playful smack on the leg. His eyes flashed as he asked to be slapped harder. At first, I thought he was joking but the look in his eyes told me otherwise. We looked in each other's eyes and I swear he was challenging me. I asked if he was sure he wanted to do this, and he said he did not trust anyone else to be his first. I felt honoured and nervous at the same time. I knew this could go horribly wrong and end our friendship, but thought we were strong enough to get past anything.

I slapped him harder this time, in the same place as before. A small murmur escaped his lips and I knew that this was what he wanted. I assumed that as I was doing the slapping that he wanted to be at my beckon call. I told him to pass my wine, which he did but replying "yes mistress". I laughed nervously. I asked if this was seriously what he wanted, he admitted to loving me for years and hated it when I was with someone else. He said it did not matter if my partner were male or female, he hated it, although when I was dating women, he could deal with that more as the competition did not feel so fierce. I was gobsmacked by this revelation as I had no idea he felt that way.

Once I had recovered from the shock of his admission, I thought that it was kind of sweet and a bit of a turn on too. I had always been a bit possessive of Rory and I guess it was because I had some feelings for him, although not as strong. I admitted this to him, and we sat there in silence for a few minutes as we processed the information. We looked at each other and laughed, both of us amazed that we felt that way but neither of us had said anything. Our eyes locked and I felt a warm feeling spread throughout me. I think he must have felt the same as we were soon kissing on the sofa. His tongue would part my lips and dart inside, and I would gently bite his lip, making him moan softly. I moved swiftly and straddled him, and he grabbed my ass and pulled me into him. My hands roughly yanked at his hair as he licked my neck. I shift my weight as I feel his cock growing beneath me and I kiss him deeply. His hands move up from my bum to my breasts and he kneaded them like dough balls. I become breathless as I get more turned on but pull away from him as I do not want this to end too soon.

I push myself off him and take his hand. He follows me to the bedroom where I tell him lie on the bed. I walk over to my dresser and open a drawer. Inside is my collection of toys and lubes. Being bi-sexual I have a variety of dildo's, vibrators, and strap on's. I pull out some lube and walk back to the bed. I ask him what he would like me to do, and he replies with whatever I like. I laugh with excitement at the prospect of being in control of him. As I approach the bed, I remove my pyjamas, leaving just my underwear on. Luckily, it is a matching set as I was not expecting this to happen tonight. My large breasts are only just enclosed by the bra and the slip of fabric that is meant to be my knickers covers virtually nothing. I watch him as he looks me up and down in appreciation. I feel a wetness creep onto the slim material and a warm rush floods my body. As I get to the bed, he has started to remove his shirt and trousers, and I help him get down to just his boxers. I gentle take his cock in my hand and start rubbing through the material of them. I feel him swell at my touch and he sighs slowly. His arms snake round my waist and he pulls me into him. He kisses my belly softly and makes his way up to my breasts which he attends to in turn. I want to take this to the next step, but I am not sure how to proceed. He senses my hesitation and looks up at me. I tell him I am ok and that I want to try something. He tells me I can do what I want. I ask him to massage my back (I want to see what he will do in this situation). He sits me down on the bed before laying me down. He gently starts rubbing my shoulders and works his way down my back. When he gets to my bra, he undoes it in one hand and whips it off with the other. He returns to my back pressing deep on any knots he finds. I feel the stress from work ease out of me as the massage continues. He works lower and lower down my back until he reaches my bum. I lift my hips to allow him to remove my pants. As he slowly rubs his hands over my buttocks, he leans forward and kisses each cheek.

He whispers that he has waited so long to do this and how much he had admired my bum from afar. His massage becomes faster and harder and I think that he is keen on my behind. His kisses get longer so much so that it seems like he is sucking on my cheeks. He quietly tells me he could do this for hours as he loves my bum. I tell him to show me how much he loves it and he parts my cheeks and blows on my hole. I contract as I was not expecting that quite so soon, and he continues to knead my buttocks and blow. A few minutes pass and I relax again, this time he strokes his finger down the crease and around my knot. I am more prepared this time and allow him to carry on. His hands slip around my waist and he gently lifted my hips, enabling him to place a pillow beneath them. As I get comfortable, I realise that this gives him better access, and I wonder what he is going to do next. I feel his warm breath and I try to relax as much as possible as he circles my sphincter with his tongue. I gasp as he slides the tip into my rectum for the first time. A shudder passes through my whole body as a wave of warmth spreads outward from there. He spent a few minutes tongue fucking my ass before inserting his fingers instead. First 1 then 2 and so on until he had 3 in. He then started pumping them in and out of me allowing a beautiful orgasm to crash over me. The sweat at this point was dripping off me and I got up on wobbly legs and headed to the bathroom to get a towel.

When I came back, I grabbed a small butt plug from my stash and hid it under the towel. I threw the towel and plug onto the bed and kissed Rory hard on the lips. I made him lay down on the bed face first and gave him a massage paying particular attention to his legs as they seemed very tense. I could hear how much he was enjoying it by the little moans that escaped his mouth. I kept grabbing his butt and squeezing, not too hard at first but getting progressively harder. Each time I grabbed him, I parted his cheeks a little, getting wider each time. I could feel him relaxing at each pass and after a while I ran my finger over his butthole. I could feel him flinch and I apologised pretending it was an accident. I kept doing it until he stopped flinching, when he did, I left my finger there a bit longer and slowly circled him. A low guttural growl left his lips and I knew he was mine. I rummaged under the towel and bought out the plug. I always kept a tube of lube beside my bed for when I woke up horny and needed to bring myself off. I carefully flicked open the lip with one hand and poured a little on the tip. I also put some on the end of my finger then swapped hands. I slowly pushed my finger into him but stopped when I felt him tighten around it. I waited until he had relaxed again, then pushed in a little further. you could hear the breath caught in his throat, and as I pulled my finger out the air escaped his mouth. I rapidly pushed it back in before he could inhale again. I did this a few times as he got into the flow of it, then whipped out my finger and replaced it with the plug. I heard a sharp intake of air as the plug was a bit bigger than my finger. And as he exhaled, I pushed it in until it was in all the way. I asked him if he was enjoying it and he grunted at me. I told him to keep the plug in his ass without the use of his hands. That boy clenched around it so hard. I shifted off the bed and went back to my drawer. I pulled out a few more plugs of varying sizes, a strap on and a riding crop and went back to the bed.

He had kept the plug right where I had left it and told him how proud I was of him. I asked he if he wanted more, to wish he mumbled that he did. I put lube on another plug and swapped them over, the noise coming from him, told me that he was staring to get used to it.

Again, I told him to hold it, which he did, and I picked up the whip and started to stroke his ass with it. He squirmed under its touch and I gently tapped his ass with it. He squirmed again, so the tap got harder. This continued a few times until there was a red welt on his cheek. He then stopped squirming as I had found his threshold. My hand gently rubbed the mark and a small whimper came from him. I left that plug in a bit longer this time to really allow him to relax into the scenario. The next time I replaced the plug it what quite a bit larger than the last, so I made sure there was plenty of lube and that he was ready for it. As I inserted the tip into his rectum, he pushed back and engulfed it all. It took me a little by surprise and I tapped him again with the whip and told him that I was in control not him. He apologised and called me mistress. This was the first time he had said it and a smile crept across my lips. He had really taken to it all really well and I believed he was prepared enough for what I had planned next. I stepped into the leather straps and did them up tightly. I told him to get on his knees and get comfortable. He looked back over his shoulder, to see what I was doing, but a crack with the whip on his ass, made him look forward and another apology came my way. I knelt behind him and stroked his cheeks and lower back. I leant forward and nudged the end against his back passage. He went to push back but stopped himself before the whip hit. I took hold of his hips and gently eased my way in. I allowed him time to adjust to the width of the dildo, before thrusting into him. A small cry came from him and I told him that he had to tell me when he was getting close to coming. He nodded his understanding and I continued to rock back and forth into him. His breath was getting ragged and I thought it would not be long before he came. I slowed down my efforts and he moaned his disappointment. A touch of the crop soon stopped the moans but then the grunts started. I decided that he had probably been through enough that night and quickened the pace. I was thrusting hard when I put my hand between his legs and grabbed his rock-hard cock. I jerked him off whilst thrusting into him and felt his balls start to tighten. I let go of his cock and went back to his hips as I pushed into him harder and harder. His moans were getting louder and I could feel him tense up as he was about to come. He let out a grunt and his hips started to buck under me. I gave him one long, hard thrust and he came violently. His jism sprayed all over my bed and down his legs before he collapsed on the bed. I slowly withdrew from his ass and handed him the towel. He lay there for a few moments before rolling over onto his back, sweat dripping from his brow. He looked at me with relief and laughed. I took of my plastic cock whilst he cleaned himself down then we lay together on the bed. He kissed me hard and thanked me over and over for a wonderful night. My reply was to say that the night was not over, this was just an interval.

Craving Pleasure

Furious, I yanked the door to the washing machine open and pulled my clothing from it, piling them into the washer immediately to the left. When I finished, I slammed the door on the first machine, before walking angrily over to the vending machine where you can buy individual laundry detergents for fifty cents. It had been a long, shitty day, and to pile all of my clothes into a machine that turned out to be broken was almost more than I could take. I was alone in the laundry mat, and slamming doors and kicking chairs out of my way as I walked back to the washing machine felt good; it was an easy way to get out some of my stress. Back at my washer I shut that door hard too, and put the soap in the top of the machine. When I attempted to toss the empty box into the trash, I overshot the bucket, infuriating me all over again. "FUCK!" I yelled in the empty room, overreacting at the missed shot. I headed over to pick up the box from the floor, and physically jumped in surprise to see a man on the other side of the washing machines loading his laundry into a dryer. How had I not known he was there?! Immediately I was embarrassed, and I mumbled an apology.

"It's ok" the man sad gruffly, and he bent to pick up the box I was about to retrieve. When he was close enough to hand me the box, I could smell the liquor on him, and for some reason I felt a little better. "Rough day, girl?" he asked me, as I tossed the box away, and I smiled a little.

"Yeah, you could say that...just long and filled with all kinds of shit," I muttered, thinking about the double shift I had just worked at the restaurant, the lack of tips I had received from a large table of lowlifes, and the fact that I was scheduled to work another double shift tomorrow, to cover for an irresponsible co-worker. "Anyway," I said to the man, who appeared to be in his 30's – probably about 10 years older than I, "I'm sorry I lost my temper, I didn't mean to make so much noise and stuff..." I let my voice trail off, not sure what else to say.

"Don't worry about it kid, you're sexy as hell when you're angry like that," he said glancing at me appreciatively and throwing me completely off guard.

"I'm – but – what?" I stammered, completely surprised that this man would be so forward, and utterly unsure how to respond.

"You look so surprised," the guy said to me, seeming surprised at this. "It's all your aggression, the ferocity in your face..." he paused for a moment, then continued, "you just look like your craving a good hard fuck." He was matter of fact about it, and I could feel myself blushing, partly because nobody had ever spoken to me like that before, and partly because, as much as I hated to admit it, it was true.

I wondered what he thought of me at that moment, with my dark brown hair up in a sloppy pony tail, and me looking like a stressed-out mess. I was wearing the only thing that was clean in my apartment – a pair of comfortable, worn in jeans, and an old, thin white tank top. I had my black bra on underneath, and I knew it was showing through, but I didn't care. I figured he couldn't tell that I didn't have on any panties, they'd simply all been in the dirty clothes basket. All of this was flashing through my head, and my thoughts were only broken when he asked me a question.

"I bet you just want to get on a cock and ride yourself to a good hard cum, don't you girl?" He asked laughing.

I surprised myself by answering quickly and honestly. "Actually buddy," I said, attitude creeping into my voice, "that's where you're wrong. I don't want to get on and ride, because that's simply too much effort." My voice was calm, even as I was screaming inside my head, wondering what the hell I was doing, discussing this with some guy in the laundry mat. "What I really need is for someone to just take control; you know, just bend me over and fuck me hard. Make me take it, make me cum, make me forget about how fucking shitty this day was." This time it was he who seemed surprised, as he looked at me, clearly wondering if I was serious or just dicking him around. And it was me that laughed this time. "I'm not kidding," I said laughing, satisfied to see him look so shocked, as I turned my back on him to pick up my laundry basket from the floor.

I bent over to pick up my laundry basket, and almost instantly, before I could straighten up again, I could feel the man behind me. I don't just mean I could sense his presence, or tell that he had moved closer, no, I mean that I could literally feel him standing behind me. He was so close that his pelvis was pressed against my ass, and I felt the heat rise to my cheeks as

I felt his dick twitch through his pants. I was surprised to feel his hand at the back of my head, even more so when he grabbed my pony tail and pulled, ordering me, without words, to straighten back up. I left my laundry basket on the floor as I stood, and when I was standing up straight again he released my pony tail and turned me around, so I was facing him.

Once again, I could smell the hint of alcohol on his breath, and as I looked at him I wondered if he were drunk. I noticed other things in that quick moment too: that he was a good looking guy; tanned, with dark brown eyes, and dark stubble studding his chin, suggesting a couple days since his last shave. He stood there, inches from my face, and grinned, and I couldn't help but grin back. His smile was a combination of little boy mischief and pure male lust, paired with a little bit of devilishness that was more suggestive than any smile I'd ever seen in my life. And as I took him in, and stood there with his hands firmly gripping my shoulders, I knew that he had listened to what I said, and that he intended to follow through. This scared me for a split second, but even more than that, it excited me, and I could feel myself getting wet.

He must have seen the brief flash of fear in my eyes, and also noticed that it faded away, because he grinned again, and said in a low voice, "little girl, you don't know what you've gotten yourself into." I tried to think of a flippant response, but had no time, because suddenly his hands on my shoulders were pushing down, pushing me down, until I was on my knees in front of him. Realizing what he wanted, I licked my lips in anticipation, having been craving a cock in my mouth for months, since my last boyfriend and I had broken up. He noticed, and laughed. "You better do a damn good job then girl," we warned, tugging my pony tail loose and wrapping one hand in my hair, while he undid his jeans with the other. The tugging on my hair was turning me on more than I ever thought it would, and I was straining against his grip trying to get closer to him as he pulled down his jeans and boxers in one quick motion. As his cock sprang free I opened my mouth eagerly, and sucked in the head, swirling my tongue around it, savoring the feeling of finally having a man in my mouth again.

His dick was bigger than any I'd ever had, a realization that came to me as I sucked on it. In an attempt to please him while easing myself into the blowjob, I reached up and gripped the base of his shaft with my hand, so that I could jerk him off while my mouth only had to tackle the first few inches of his cock. I savored it, going slow, then speeding up a little, until suddenly the guy slapped my hand away, hard. "Nice try girl," he said harshly, "but I don't want a fucking hand job. I want you to use that pretty mouth and swallow my dick, and if you can't do it on your own, then I'm gonna help you." He didn't sound mad, exactly, but it was clear that he knew what he wanted, so I tried to take him a little deeper. He was so big and thick though, that I struggled, and had to back off again almost immediately. I was sucking hard on the head of his dick, eliciting a groan from him, when, without warning, his hand tightened hard in my hair, and he pushed my head forward, forcing me to take a little more than half of his cock all at once. I felt my throat stretching, and almost instantly I was gagging, my throat constricting around him. He pulled my head back off his cock just as forcefully as he had pushed it forward, letting me focus again on just the head. I caught my breath in a big gasp of air, and then he was pushing me forward again, this time I took another inch or so before gagging hard, and once again he pulled me back. Again I gasped for breath, again he pushed me forward. As I gagged around his thickness the third time, I could feel my pussy clenching, my clit throbbing for attention. It occurred to me, as he was mercifully pulling me away from his cock once again, that the feeling of being forced to swallow him was turning me on. He seemed to read my mind, because he laughed as he pushed me forward again, saying "You like that, don't you girl? You like it when I make you choke on my big cock don't you? It's making you hot, making you want me to fuck you, isn't it?" I groaned around his cock that was almost all the way in my mouth, only about one inch that I hadn't managed to swallow yet. That wasn't good enough for him though, he wanted me to actually answer him. He jerked my head and pulled me away hard, "Answer me, little girl, you like having me fuck your throat like this?" He used my hair to tilt my head, make me look up at him. My eyes were watering and my throat was spasming, but I let out a garbled yes, and then shocked him by plunging my own head forward, and swallowing his whole cock, on my own. "Fuuuuck, that's a good girl," I could hear him groaning above me, and even as I gagged his words were having an effect on me. I ground the back of my throat against the head of his cock, feeling my lips pressed against his crotch. He tried to pull me back off to let me breathe, but I didn't want to, I loved the feeling of him filling my throat. He tugged my hair harder, and harder still, until finally I had to obey and back off, feeling my scalp tingle from the pulling. I gasped for air, surprised to realize I needed it so badly, and then he forced me back on his dick hard, causing me to gag again in surprise, and moan in pleasure. I reached up with my hand and squeezed his balls, while I sucked on the cock deep in my throat. I snuck my tongue out at the base of his dick, and teased the edge of his balls with it, causing his hand to tighten hard in my hair, while he jerked his hips forward and ground his dick deeper, making me feel like I would actually swallow it. Suddenly, almost with urgency, he pulled me away again, hard, this time all the way off of his cock. He still held my hair, and I was still kneeling, while he looked down at me in surprise. He was breathing heavy, and I suddenly realized that I must have almost made him cum, that's why he made me stop. "You're one amazing little cock sucker, kid," he said between breaths, looking surprised and immensely pleased.

Still using my hair to direct me, he pulled me to my feet until I was standing in front of him. He turned me around, so my back was to him, and pulled me tight against him; I could feel his hard cock pulsing against my ass through my jeans. One hand still in my hair, he jerked my head to the side a little, making me tilt it, exposing my neck. Instantly his mouth was on it, kissing and sucking. When he nibbled a little bit I let out a small moan, and then he bit me harder, just below my ear, causing my knees to almost buckle with the pleasure and pain that mixed together. "Mmmm, like that, girl, when I bite you?" he asked, in his low voice, while his hand squeezed my breast hard over my shirt. He took his other hand away from my hair and used them both to pull my thin tank top quickly up and over my head. It suddenly occurred to me, as my shirt hit the floor, that we were there, in the laundry mat, he naked from the waist down, and me in jeans and my bra (not knowing how long either would stay on). I started to protest, mentioning that we were in a public building, but my words turned to a groan when he bit down hard on my collar bone, causing me to involuntarily grind back into him. "It's almost 1:00 in the morning, kid," he said quietly, "it's just me and you here." I thought about arguing more, my good sense told me I should, but as he kissed my neck hard, and dragged his teeth up to my earlobe, my good sense went out the window. He was biting my ear, and then teasing it with his tongue as he unhooked my bra and let that fall to the floor near my shirt. As soon as it was gone his hands replaced it, his fingers immediately finding my swollen nipples and squeezing them. He wasted no time being with gentle, pinching and tugging them as I ground against him. I yelped when he pulled them both hard, causing him to pinch them too, and even through the pain I could feel my pussy getting soaked as my body craved more. "You said you wanted it hard," he warned, "And I'm gonna give you exactly what you wanted." He paused for a moment, licking my ear as he pinched my nipples even harder, the combination of pleasure and pain making me squirm against him and moan desperately for more. "Ooooh you like that, don't you? You love it when I pinch those nipples and make them hurt a little bit..." he blew in my ear, then whispered, "There's more where that came from." He let up on one nipple, but pinched the other harder, causing the free one to throb and crave his painful attentions again.

I was so focused on the feelings in my nipples and my neck where he kept alternating between kissing and biting, that I almost didn't even notice when his hand slipped over my stomach and into the front of my jeans. All at once he stopped everything; his hands paused exactly where they were. "You little slut!" he whispered, surprised, in my ear. "You're not even wearing panties under these jeans..."his voice trailed off for a moment and he slid his hand lower into my jeans, sliding a finger between my pussy lips, "and you're cunt's fucking soaked!" He flicked his finger hard across my clit, causing me let out a cry of pleasure, and he brought his other hand away from my chest and down to undo my jeans. "No fucking panties," he pondered, "and a pussy shaved completely smooth...you're just dying for a pounding, aren't you?"

With that he pushed me forward, bending me over one of the many counters where customers would usually fold their clothes. By then, every nerve in my body was on fire, between his words, and the way he had hurt my nipples and my neck, making the pleasure he offered that much more exquisite. I was dying for him to fuck me, and he knew it, and I knew it was coming. I braced myself for the thickness of his cock, knowing that it would stretch my pussy like none ever had before. Instead though, I suddenly felt his fingertip, just one, teasing my pussy lips. I looked back, to see him kneeling on the floor behind me. For a split second I was disappointed, I wanted him to fuck me, and hard! Something must have tipped him off, for he stood up, and slapped my ass hard, making it sting. He leaned over close to me and looked at me carefully. "Listen to me, girl," he said, in a voice that meant business. "Just because I'm not holding you down right now, doesn't mean that you have permission to move. You're going to stand there, and take whatever I give you. And if I tease you, and believe me, I'm going to; you're going to endure it." He paused, and slapped my ass again, the sharp sting mixing with a tingle as he ran his fingertips slowly over the reddened area. "I know you want me to fuck your brains out, and I'm going to, you can count on that. But you also said you wanted someone else to be in charge...so that's exactly what you're gonna get kid. I'm in charge, and that means you don't get fucked until I'm ready to fuck you, got it?" He slapped my ass again, and I groaned, but when I didn't answer he grabbed my hair and jerked my head. "Got it?" he demanded.

"Yes," I said weakly, as he moved away from me and slapped my ass, one more time, hard. He moved behind me again, and again teased my pussy with his fingertip. I could feel him slipping it between my lips, and stroking slowly back and forth, gently around my opening, teasing it. When I tried to push against his finger, wanting to feel it slide hard inside me, he reached up with his free hand and slapped my ass hard, reminding me that I was not in charge. I whimpered, my ass cheek now on fire from the repeated slaps, sure that there must be a red welt forming. Still he teased me with that one finger, and if I'd thought it couldn't get any worse, I was wrong. When his finger found my clit he passed over it very gently, making a large circle around it, but not concentrating any intense pleasure on the throbbing little bud itself. I could feel my pulse throbbing everywhere throughout my body; feel my pussy aching for release that this man wouldn't give me. I let out a groan of frustration; my face pressed against the counter still, and was suddenly rewarded when he pinched my clit hard. It was a sharp, intense pleasure, almost painful, and it did turn painful when he twisted it, then, just as quickly he released it and stroked it with his finger tip, almost making me cum. He stopped just before I could, and he laughed.

"Soon, little girl," he promised me, as he slid his finger into my pussy in one quick motion. I could feel myself clenching at his finger, my pussy literally begging him not to take it out, but of course he did. He immediately replaced it though, with two fingers, which forced my tight cunt to stretch a bit to accommodate them. I let out a sigh of pleasure at the feeling of being filled, finally, and pushed against his fingers eagerly as he twisted them inside me. He quickly found my gspot and stroked it hard, making my knees shake, and my hands grip at the counter against the intense pleasure that none of my boyfriends had ever mastered the art of supplying. His fingers felt so good that I almost didn't feel his tongue at first, as he licked around his fingers, teasing the opening, then sucking on my pussy lips. Then he licked forward and when his tongue found my clit I let out a loud moan that I just couldn't contain. "Mmm, you like that girl?" he asked as he tongued my clit, then sucked it hard between his lips. When his teeth grazed it I felt myself buck against his face, could feel myself on the brink of an orgasm.

"I need to...I'm gonna..." my voice trailed off as I felt my orgasm approaching, but suddenly he stopped everything, his fingers motionless inside me, his face just inches from my pussy.

"No, you're not," he said, refusing to give me any more attention for over a minute, making me want to cry with disappointment. "I'm going to let you cum like this," he said calmly, "but not until I'm ready. Understand?" He was talking to me from his spot beneath me, and feeling like I couldn't take it anymore I tried to grind against his fingers that were still buried inside me. Instantly there was a hard slap on my ass as he stood up. He grabbed my hair with one hand and pulled me away from the counter, his fingers on his other hand still in deep in my aching pussy. "Now you're not going to get anymore attention until you swallow my cock again," he ordered, and with that, he jerked me down to my knees, and forward, and forced his whole cock into my throat in one hard fast motion, while he took his fingers from my pussy, leaving it feeling completely empty. He held the back of my head with both hands and fucked my mouth like nobody ever had before, pulling almost all the way out on each stroke, then thrusting back in, until the head slammed into the back of my throat. The feeling of complete submission overtook me as he did this, and made me just as hot as everything else he'd done. Feeling desperate for release, I reached down and played with my own clit, stroking it, while he fucked my mouth. He noticed, and I felt him thicken and jerk in the back of my throat. "Mmmm, that's right, play with yourself while you blow me," he groaned, "But don't you dare fucking cum, got it?" To obey him, I had to slow down on my clit, touching it gently, and circling it slowly, the way he had done earlier to tease me. Even then, the pleasure of my touch combined with the feeling of him using my mouth was almost too much. A few moments later though, he withdrew, his cock rock hard and huge.

He pulled me up again, and pushed me back into the same position, bent over the counter. "Now if I play with you," he asked me, "You're not going to try to cum, are you? Not until I say so, right?" I promised I wouldn't, desperate to feel his touch again, trusting that he would eventually let me cum. He returned to kneeling between my legs, and he started licking me, sucking on my clit gently, then stroking his tongue along the opening of my now drenched pussy. He licked back up to my clit, then back down, this time passing my pussy and licking all the way back to my asshole. I let out a gasp of surprise and pleasure, having never had anyone touch, let alone lick my ass before. Back and forth he licked, over and over, and each time he hit my clit or asshole with his tongue my whole body shook with a jolt of pleasure. He worked diligently on my clit for a few moments, and eased his two fingers back into my pussy, which I immediately pushed back against, but not in an attempt to cum, as I knew that would only get me into trouble. Instead I just ground against them, enjoying the pressure on my gspot, while he licked and sucked my clit. I was surprised when suddenly I felt a pressure and a tickle against my asshole, and realized that he was stroking it with his finger tip.

"Nobody's ever - " I started to object, but he chose that moment to suck on my clit, hard, and I said no more. He continued licking and sucking, alternating between the two, while stroking in and out of my pussy with his two fingers. He slid a third finger into me, and I groaned, gripping the table, feeling stretched more than I ever had in my life. "You almost ready to cum, pretty girl?" he asked me, immediately flicking my clit with his tongue after speaking. Suddenly he started stroking my gspot harder, pressing his fingers against it and letting me grind on them hard, while licking my clit furiously. He grazed his teeth across it, and then sucked hard, and as my body filled with incredible pleasure he slowly pushed the finger from his other hand deep into my ass. I'd almost forgotten it was there, and suddenly feeling it sliding into me, into a place where nobody had ever touched, was almost more than I could bear. He pulled it out slowly, eliciting a whole new series of sensations, and causing me to whimper when it was gone. Then he slammed it back in hard, and suddenly he was fucking my ass with his finger while he sucked hard on my clit and stroked my gspot with the fingers of the other hand. I couldn't take it anymore and my body started to shake and tremble. "That's it, good girl," he coaxed, "it's time to cum now, all over my hand and my face...a nice hard cum..." and with that he bit and sucked on my clit even harder, seemed to push his fingers even deeper, and my whole body clenched. I could feel my pussy and ass clamping around his fingers, could feel myself flooding this guy with my juice, and there was nothing I could do to stop it. It was the most intense orgasm I'd ever had in my life, and as I came down from it, I realized I was using the counter to support myself.

He stood, and bent over the counter next to me. He grinned at me, and I smiled back. Without warning, he pulled my face to his and kissed me, deep, our tongues colliding. I could taste my own cum on his lips and tongue, and although I had just had an incredible orgasm, I could feel myself responding to this kiss from this stranger, and already wanting more again. He had taken off his shirt at some point, and now he pulled me to him, my tits grazing his chest; I could feel his muscles against me. I arched back, pressing my hips to his, feeling his cock, still hard and huge, pressing against my pelvis, just a little above my pussy. "That was incredible," I whispered, looking up at him in awe.

"Glad you enjoyed it," he said grinning, "But I hope you realize that we're not done...I haven't even given you what you wanted yet." With that, he turned me back around, and pressed me back down over the counter. He slapped my ass again, this time the other cheek, and held my back down with his hand while he repeated the spanking several times. "Can't have one cheek all red and sore and the other perfectly white," he said laughing a little, before spanking me again, causing me to whimper. "Don't even try to tell me you don't like this, girl," he said, his voice gruff again, like it had been earlier. "After every slap your ass jumps back towards my hand like it's craving another one, see?" And with that he whacked it again, and indeed, I felt my ass jump off the table, trying to push back into his hand. I blushed, embarrassed, causing him to laugh. "It's ok kid," he said, "to like pain. And I can tell you do...you liked me biting you, pinching your nipples, using my teeth on your clit..." his voice trailed off and I felt incredibly embarrassed. He came up close behind me, his dick pressing against my ass as he bent over me, conspiratorially. "It's good that you like it to hurt a little..." he said quietly in my ear, "Because I think we both know that when I fuck you, in a just minute, it's definitely going to hurt..." His voice trailed off and I felt a thrill run up my spine. He backed up a little, and spread my legs open wider, as he held me bent over the counter still. Instead of fucking me right then though, he spanked me again, right in the middle of my ass, making both of my cheeks throb and sting, making me buck against the table. He slapped me again and again, each time his hand seeming to make contact a little lower, until suddenly, one of his slaps struck me half on the ass, half on my pussy. It made me jump and yelp, even more so when he did it again. Each time his hand made contact with my pussy though, despite the sting, I could feel myself getting wetter and hornier. Without even realizing what I was doing, I was suddenly begging for his cock, spreading my legs wider to allow him more access to my pussy for each slap, willing to do anything that would get him to fuck me sooner.

And I was rewarded. The spanking stopped and he moved in closer, my legs still spread wide, and my ass presented to him as I stood bent over the counter. "Reach back and open yourself up for me, if you want me to fuck you good and hard," he ordered, and immediately I did as I was told, reaching back and pulling my pussy open for him. "Good girl," he said, as he slowly slid half of his cock into me. My eyes widened as I felt myself stretching, much wider than I had for his three fingers. I'd been preparing for it to hurt, but not like that. It was so tight, it hurt worse than the first time I'd ever had sex.

"Please go slow," I begged him, but he did just the opposite, pulling out and pushing half of his thick cock back in quickly.

"You never said anything about wanting it slow, honey," he said, as he pulled all the way out again and just teased the opening of my pussy with the head of his cock for a moment. He pushed in the head, making me stretch around the thickest part of the ridge, letting me adjust to it, then pulling it back out, making me stretch around it again. He did this over and over, sometimes slow, and sometimes fast, until slowly the pain started to dissipate as my pussy began to crave more than just the head. The next time he pushed the head in, I pushed back against him, making him give me just a little more. I caught him off guard and managed to get a couple of satisfying inches, but then he held back the rest. "I thought you wanted me to go slow now," he teased. "You're just never satisfied are you?" Before I could answer he pushed back into me, this time hard and fast, slamming his entire cock deep into my pussy.

"Fuck!" I screamed into my arm, muffling the sound as I felt myself being stretched in every direction around his massive pole. He leaned over and kissed my neck, sucking, as he'd done earlier. He kissed down to my shoulder, while he pulled slowly out, then bit hard as he slammed back in. The duel sensations of pain, tinged with pleasure made me incredibly wet again, and I couldn't help but push back against him, grinding into his thick cock. He reached around with one hand and started stroking my clit hard, while he continued to pull his cock all the way out and force it back in deep, but now I was pushing back to meet each of his thrusts, loving the feeling of being impaled with each stroke. With his free hand he grabbed my hair in his fist, forcing me to arch back with each thrust, especially when I tried to push my ass back to meet his stroke, making me take him even deeper still.

Suddenly he slid in deep all the way, and ground hard against me, and didn't pull away. He bent over me from behind like he'd done earlier. "You're loving that thick cock fucking you're cunt, aren't you?" he groaned against my ear. I nodded yes, grinding my ass back against him, craving more. "You ready to take it in that tight little ass of yours, girl?" he asked me, and I felt myself tighten around him in both excitement and terror. The only thing I'd ever had in my ass was his finger, and that was tight. I couldn't imagine what it would feel like to have his cock there, how badly it would hurt. On the other hand, having his finger there earlier had given me the most incredible orgasm of my life. "It doesn't really matter if you're ready or not," he said when I didn't answer him, as he slowly pulled away and withdrew his cock. "Because I'm ready, so you're going to take it."

With that being said, he pulled me away from the counter and turned me around. "I figure you must be getting sick of that position," he said laughing, "and although I know you said you wanted to be bent over and fucked hard, I think you'll like this just as much." He took my hand and brought me over to another counter, on the other side of the laundry mat, one that was slightly lower than the first. Immediately he picked me up and set me down onto it, so I was sitting on the edge. I couldn't help but notice that I was almost perfectly lined up with his cock at this height. "Now lay back," he ordered, and he guided me backwards firmly, until I was laying down, flat on my back. "Pull your legs up and hold onto them, otherwise I'll have to find something in your laundry to tie them up with, got it, girl?"

Obediently, I pulled my legs up, spread, and held my knees tightly, feeling incredibly exposed and open in the position. I could feel the cool air on my pussy and my asshole, and started to feel very nervous about taking his dick in my ass. Just as I was about to lower my legs and object, I felt his fingers running carefully over my pussy, stroking and teasing my clit, then slipping slowly into my pussy. I was surprised, since I'd been expecting something entirely different, but didn't complain when he started pumping in and out of my pussy with two fingers. At this angle he could finger me nice and deep, and he managed to hit my gspot with every stroke. In less than a minute I was groaning and writhing on the table, and could feel my wetness flooding my pussy, overflowing it and running between my ass cheeks. Suddenly I felt my pussy stretching again, and realized that he had quickly replaced his fingers with his cock once again, but at that moment it felt so good that I could barely remember how badly it had hurt earlier. I lifted my hips eagerly, pushing into his cock, silently begging for more, and at that exact moment, as he thrust in all the way, he also slid two fingers deep into my ass. By that time it was soaking wet from all of my juice, so his fingers went in relatively easily, surprising me as I could feel myself being stuffed even fuller than before. He fingered my ass for a few minutes while pounding my pussy with his dick, and ordered me to reach down and play with my own clit for him. "I want to see you play with that little clit of yours while I fuck you," he instructed, "I want to feel you clench around me each time your finger hits is." I was more than happy to oblige him, and did, stroking my clit slowly and enjoying the feeling of being fucked in both holes at the same time.

Without warning he pulled his cock from my pussy, leaving me feeling very empty. I let out a whimper, and a second later he pulled his fingers out of my ass, leaving me feeling emptier still. Before I could protest that though, I felt him quickly press the head of his cock against my ass and push, forcing me to open around the head of his cock. It hurt, a lot more than I expected, and I started begging him to stop, that it hurt too much, that I wasn't ready. "Just play with your clit, little girl, keep making that feel nice, because I'm going to fuck your ass, and you're gonna end up loving it," he said to me, as he pushed his cock a little deeper. I tried to obey his instructions, and focused on pleasuring my clit, but I couldn't ignore that my ass was stretching painfully wider and wider around his giant dick. As he pushed in a little deeper he slid one finger into my pussy and easily found my gspot yet again, stroking it slowly. This pleasure helped me to relax almost instantly, and made it easier for him to ease more of his cock into my tight ass.

He'd been inching in deeper and deeper, when suddenly I realized that although it didn't feel good yet, my ass didn't really hurt anymore. Each time he moved the sensation was intense, still stretched tight, but it was starting to tingle and feel a little better. Suddenly he leaned forward on me, and pulled me up a little, impaling my ass as he leaned in. I let out a groan of pain, but when I looked down and saw his cock, buried completely in my ass, the groan of pain turned to a gasp of surprise and a moan of pleasure. "You like seeing that big cock all the way up your tight little ass, girl?" he asked me, while he kept fingering me. I was stroking my clit hard now and grinding against his finger, which also made me press harder against his cock. I nodded, and he pulled himself out slowly, almost all the way out, until just the head was still partially inside. He watched me, while I watched his cock slowly slide all the way back inside my ass, inch by inch. The sight of it seemed to flip a switch in my head, it was the hottest thing I'd ever seen, and I suddenly wanted to feel him fuck me there.

I lay back flat again, and pulled my legs up higher, spreading them even wider. "Fuck my ass with that cock," I begged him, the first time I'd really specified what I wanted. "Please...pound my ass with it, like you did to my pussy earlier." He looked down at me as he started to pull out again and then slide back in, with a little more speed this time.

"And what about your little cunt, hmm? What should I do with that...?" he asked, and even as he questioned me he gave it a slap as he had earlier, only this time his hand made complete stinging contact with my pussy lips and my clit. I moaned and pushed up against him, against the hand he had spanked me with and against the cock he was using to fuck my ass.

"Spank it, fuck it with your fingers, anything, please..."I was begging loud now, bucking against him, "Just do it hard, make it hurt like before, make me cum hard because it feels so good and it hurts so bad, pleeeease..."

He smiled his devilish smile and slammed his cock into my ass, and just as he buried it completely to the hilt he slapped my pussy again, harder this time. The he stroked my clit hard as he pulled his cock almost all the way out, before slamming it back in and slapping my pussy again. He repeated this over and over, spanking my pussy hard as he fucked my ass, then stroking my clit as he pulled away. At some point my hand had fallen away from my clit, but when he stopped spanking me and told me to play with myself again, I obeyed. Then, as he fucked my ass hard, he slipped first two, then almost immediately three fingers deep into my pussy, finger fucking me in rhythm with his cock in my ass.

"You like being fucked in both holes, don't you, girl?" he asked, gazing down at me with that grin. "I bet you're imagining two big cocks right now aren't you, one in your wet little pussy, and another in that tight little ass..." His voice trailed off as he fucked me harder, and I stroked my clit hard, occasionally pinching it as he had done, intensifying the pleasure. I was teetering on the edge of an orgasm, when suddenly he managed to slide another finger deep into my pussy with the first three, stretching me out even more, making my pussy and ass feel tighter than I ever thought possible. All at once he pushed in deep with his cock and his fingers, forcing me to grind on both of them. I couldn't take anymore, with one final pinch of my clit I started cumming, tightening around his fingers and cock, and almost instantly I could feel his cock thicken and jerk deep in my ass, and I knew he was cumming deep inside my ass. That thought seemed to only make me cum harder, and my body shook and trembled on the counter, ground as tightly against him as I could possibly get. Even after he finished, and was slowly easing his cock out of my ass, I could feel little aftershock spasms jerking my body, making my pussy clench around his retreating fingers.

As I sat up I realized I was dizzy, and I grinned sheepishly as he helped me down from the counter. I excused myself to go to the bathroom and cleaned up, and when I came out, he went in. I switched my clothes into the dryer, and tried to wrap my head around what I had just done. My thoughts were broken by his voice when he returned from the bathroom.

"Feel better?" he asked me, smiling, and I couldn't help but laugh when I nodded.

"Yes, I think that was exactly what I needed," I smiled, a little embarrassed, but feeling genuinely better.

He walked over to the dryer where his clothes were and loaded them into a basket nearby. I couldn't help but wonder how long they'd been done for, while we'd been busy doing other activities.

"I should probably get going..." he said, his basket of clean laundry in his hand. He looked away for a minute, then back at me. "But, well, just so you know, I always do my laundry at this time on Friday nights...." For a brief second, he looked unsure of himself, something that shocked me since he had taken such control earlier. "So, you know, maybe we'll see each other again." He grinned, and I nodded.

"Yeah, I wouldn't be surprised...it's nice doing laundry at this time of night." I grinned back at him, and waved as he walked out the door. Then I grabbed my notepad from my bag and started writing down the encounter, wanting to share it. And even as I wrote about it, I could feel myself getting wet again as I relived the evening, and even wetter as I wondered at all the things that could happen next time.

TABOO SEX STORIES FOR ADULTS

Explicit Dirty Taboo Collection: Lesbian, BDSM, Romantic Intense and Forbidden Desires, Hot Stories And Much More...

Jenna Grey

Complete Bliss

I wait for him on my knees, right in front of the door. I'm totally naked. My blonde hair that falls down my back in lazy curls. I have a collar around my neck, adorned with metal studs. It's connected to a leash trailing down my body. I'm holding it myself for now. But I know my master will come soon, and take it from my hands.

He might pull me behind to the bedroom, while I crawl on all fours. Then he would use me. I imagine his hard cock inside me, filling me. I imagine how it might taste it my mouth. How it would feel in my ass.

I'm so wet. This is really hard. I can feel my juices trickling down my thighs. I need him so bad.

I pull on the leash myself, and imagine it's his grip behind it. I grab one of my small breasts, squeezing it hard, moaning.

He told me I could touch myself, as long as I didn't cum. But he also said that he would be proud of me if I could resist.

And I want to resist. I want to tell him that I didn't touch myself at all, that I waited patiently for his cock, like a good fuck slave. I smile at the thought. I bite my lip, and determinately clasp my hands behind my back to keep myself from disappointing him. But it's really hard.

When he finally comes home, he opens the door wide, letting me see the empty hallway behind him - and potentially letting anyone see me, naked and leashed, my hands clasped behind my back. There's no one, of course. It disappoints me a little. For a moment, I want everyone to see what a dirty slut I am.

My master is really tall and broad shouldered. He has short, dark hair that sets off the angular planes of his face, and a close-trimmed beard. He's wearing a nice slim-fitting button-down, with the topmost button undone, exposing his delicious collar-bones. My eyes catch on those, and I start undressing him in my mind. I swallow.

I crawl to him, on my hands and knees, and clutch at his trousers before he even closes the door. "Sir," I say, my voice carrying into the hallway with ease, "please use me. I didn't touch myself at all. I waited for your cock. Please."

He casually strokes my hair as he closes the door. "Good girl," he says. "You're such a whore, I didn't think you could do it. It was hard, wasn't it?"

Master has a confident way about him. He's not showy or obnoxious. But it's like... he has a calm certainty, of himself and his place in the world. Sometimes, I envy him for it. But mostly, it makes me proud to be his property.

"Yes, sir," I say. "I... I leaked over the floor again," I say, because I know he likes to know how wet I got waiting for him.

He smiles down at me. "That's even better," he says. "Now, come here pet," he says, and grabs my leash.

I crawl on all fours behind him. He pulls hard, and I can't crawl very fast, so the collar ends up choking me a little.

He pulls me to the living room. It's a large room with a huge window on one side. We're on the 22nd floor, so you can't see really far from here. Being naked in front of the window always gives me a thrill, even though it's unlikely anyone can see us.

He sets his bag down, and starts stroking my hair. I look up to him with wide, innocent eyes.

"Now, pet, I want you to spread your legs and show me how wet you are. Can you do that for me?"

"Y-Yes, sir," I say. Because I want him to see. I want him to know how desperate I am for him.

I sit back on my ass on the carpet and spread my thighs. I look up at him. He stiffens a little, and catches my eye. I can tell that he likes it, and I smile.

I reach down between my legs and spread my pussy for him, letting him see the glistening pinkness inside. I can almost see him getting harder.

I want him to unzip his pants and pull his cock out. I want it in my mouth. My fingers gently stroke my pussy, right at the edges, and I moan.

"God," he says quietly. "You look like such a perfect slut."

"Y-Yes, sir," I say. "Thank you."

"Stay like that," he says, and pulls out his phone. He points the camera at me, and my eyes widen. He's... going to take a picture of me. Like this. I bite my lip, but... I don't move.

"Is there something wrong, pet?" He asks, a note of warning in his voice, daring me to defy him.

"N-No, sir," I say with a small voice. "Nothing is wrong,"

I'm blushing. But I'm also spreading my legs wider for the camera, and looking into it as he takes the picture. I want to touch myself even more now. My pussy is begging for it. In front of the camera, I'm even wetter than I was before.

"Good girl," he says. He takes another one for good measure

I wonder what he's going to do with the picture. Several possibilities flit through my mind. Maybe he'll show them to his friends, so they can see what a slut his girlfriend is. Maybe he'll post them online. He might send them to the result of the faculty, to show how far I am from the woman I pretend to be.

Those things would be bad... wouldn't they? Then why does thinking about them make me feel so... good?

"Do you want to see how much of a slut you are?" He asks.

"Yes, sir," I say. Maybe he won't show the picture to anyone after all.

He flips the phone over and shows it to me. I look... even worse than I thought. My face is all flushed, my lips parted, like I'm panting. Like I'm in heat. Seeing myself like that makes me feel... 'base' might be the right word. Like... I'm at rock bottom and I don't owe anyone anything. It's not really something I can describe through words. But it feels a little like freedom.

"When you look at this picture, what do you see?" He asks me.

I pause for a moment, not knowing what to say. But then, I have it. "A dirty slut, sir," I say with excitement.

"Good girl. You're just a dirty little slut. My dirty little slut."

"Yes, yes, sir! Thank you, sir!" Because I want to be a dirty slut. His dirty slut.

He smiles. "Now, let's take some more pictures," he says. And I can't help feeling a little excited.

"Grab one of your breasts," he says. I pose for the camera, and he takes another shot.

"Do you know what I'm going to do with the pictures?" he asks, after a few more.

"No, sir," I say. I try to seem disinterested; I try to pretend they're his pictures and he can do whatever he wants with them. And I'm his property anyway. But I really want to know.

"I'm going to post them online. That way everyone will know what a dirty whore you really are. Everyone. Your students, our neighbors..." he takes another shot.

I don't move. My face just gets hotter and hotter. I cross my legs a little, because I feel a kind of heat between them too.

"R-Really?" I ask. I'm rubbing my legs together. I'm leaking again.

He doesn't answer. He just takes another shot.

"Sir?" I ask, my voice shaking, "will you really do that?"

He smiles. "Of course. Does that mean you want to stop?"

I bite my lip and say nothing.

"Maybe if you beg me enough, I won't show them to anyone," he continues.

I look away. My face is so hot. I bet I look like a tomato.

He chuckles. "But you're enjoying this, aren't you? Admit it. You're getting even wetter just thinking about what I just said."

I'm biting my lip really painfully now. I feel so ashamed.

"Pet, admit it," he says.

"...Yes, sir," I say quietly.

"Full sentences. Just 'yes' isn't enough."

"I... I want you to show the pictures," I blurt out.

"Good girl. Why do you want that?"

"I... because... I want everyone to see what a dirty slut I am," I say in a small voice. "That I'm your slut. That way... I won't... have to pretend anymore. I... it... I know it doesn't make sense."

"That's alright," he says softly, "I understand. I also want everyone to see what a slut you are. That you're my slut. That I own you," he says.

"Thank you, sir," I say. "Is... Is it really alright, though?"

"Of course, it is," he says, and strokes my hair.

"Sir?" I say.

"What is it, pet?"

"Could we take some more pictures? Please?"

He doesn't say anything at first. Just strokes my hair. For a second, I think he might refuse me. He's done that before.

"Let's do that," he finally says, a note of strain in his voice. He clears his throat. "Stand up, pet," he tells me.

I bounce up to my feet, eager to please him.

"Bend over for me and spread your ass cheeks," he says, and I do it. He takes a few shots of me like that, my holes totally exposed.

"I really love you like this, pet," he says. "Don't move yet,"

"I won't, sir," I say.

I look behind my back and see him approaching me. I think I know what's coming. And I want to ask him for it before he does it.

"Sir, please, spank me," I say.

He smiles. Then I feel his palm against my ass. I jump. He's... really strong. And he spanks really well. I try to be quiet, but I still let out an involuntary squeal.

"Now, what do you say, pet?"

"Th-Thank you, sir!" I yell breathlessly. "Again, please?"

He spanks me again. "Th-thank—"I begin, but he spanks me before I get to finish and I cry out again.

My ass burns and tingles from his palm. It's a good pain.

Then he spanks my other ass cheek, again and again. The last few smacks are really hard, but I manage to stifle everything but a tiny moan.

"Thank you, sir," I say again, breathing hard.

"You're welcome, pet," he says. Then he takes a few more photos of my ass. I hope there's a nice big palm print, so everyone will know I belong to him. His hand lingering over my ass for a moment, feeling it in his strong hand.

Then he comes really close, and presses his crotch against my ass. My stomach tightens. I feel his cock, so hard, right between my ass cheeks. It feels warm, even though the fabric of his trousers.

"Do you want me to use your ass today, pet?" He asks.

"Yes, sir!" I reply.

He licks his finger and presses it against my asshole. I'm already loose for him. I'm always loose for him.

The tip of his finger slides inside me, and I moan. He moves it in and out, gently, and I rock my hips back and forth. It's good. But... it's not enough. I need his cock. I need it to fill me.

"Please, sir," I beg. "Use my ass."

"Slut, I'm going to fuck your ass. I'm going to cum inside you. You're just such a whore that I can't help myself anymore. But you're not allowed to cum. Do you understand that?"

"Yes, sir!" I say, excited. I don't care about not Cumming. I just want him inside me. "Please—" I start begging again, but I squeal when he grabs my hair. He pulls me up and against him, making me arch my back, pressing my ass tighter against his cock.

He kisses my neck. He bites it, his teeth almost piercing the skin. I can feel his hot breath on my ear. He whispers to me, his voice rough and aggressive. "You are so fucking hot. I went hard the second I saw you, the second I opened the door. I love how much of a slut you are. How soaking wet you get. Everything you do turns me on so much."

His words fill me with warmth, all the more so for being unexpected. I moan and grind against him. I should say something. How much I love being his. How much I love his cock. How it makes me feel. But... at that moment, I just feel selfish.

"Sir, please," I whisper. "My ass. I need it." And I do. It feels as though there is an absence in me that only he can fill.

"I'll be right back, pet. Don't move," he whispers back.

He disappears into our bedroom for a moment, leaving me a little colder and lonelier without him, and comes back with a bottle of lube we keep there. I kind of feel myself loosening right when I see it.

Then he unzips his pants and slides them down, revealing his deliciously hard cock. He's so hard for me. And he's going to use me like this, without even bothering to take his clothes off.

He bends me over, and I try to push myself against a wall. It's a really uncomfortable position. He spanks me again, as though my exposed ass is too much for him to resist.

He covers two fingers with lube. I spread my cheeks for him and moan when I feel his fingers slide in. I'm so loose for him. He pushes them in deeper. I moan. He fucks me with his fingers a little more, getting me ready. Not that I need it.

He covers his cock with lube. And then I can feel it, so hot, pressing against my asshole. "Sir," I say, my voice quivering, "Please." I spread myself wider for him. But he stays there. I can feel him twitching against my asshole. His hands are on my body, exploring it. They make me tingle.

I can't help myself anymore. I need him in me. I don't care if I get punished. I push back, and he groans. He's so hard. I can feel the head of his cock stretching me, so hot against the sensitive opening.

"Oh, god," he groans. And then he slides into me.

Yes. God. Yes.

He's... he feels so big inside me. And he's so hot. It's so good.

He's breathing hard. He kisses my neck again. I want him to move. I want him to use me. He grabs my hair, making me arch my beck again. And he pushes himself deeper, so deep. I can feel his thighs against my ass. Shaking, I cry out.

"M-more," I manage, breathless.

"You're such a greedy slut," he whispers back, his voice rough and wild and so fucking hot. "I love you like this."

"Thank you, s, —"I start, but then he starts fucking my ass, and I can't speak anymore.

He goes slowly at first. Thrusting himself deep inside me, as deep as I can take. And then he goes deeper still. His hand is in my hair, and he pulls me back with every thrust. He's so strong. I'm like nothing to him. He can do whatever he wants with me.

I feel him pushing his cock into me, pounding me. I can feel his entire length sliding into me. Again. And again. And again.

Then he goes faster, and it does start to burn. But it feels so good too. He spanks me as he fucks my ass. I love it. I want him to cum. I want him to fill me up. I'm so on edge, his orgasm seems like it would be my own.

I reach out behind my back, so touch him, to feel his body, even though his clothes.

And the sounds he makes as he fucks me. God. The sounds. They reach down and ignite something within me. Or more like, stoke the fires that are already there.

"You're so fucking tight," he whispers. "God, I want to cum inside your ass. Would you like that?"

"Y-Yes," I manage between moans. I want to say more. I want to tell him how much I want it. But I can't. I don't seem to have enough words.

And then, after a few thrusts, I suddenly feel him go even harder. Even hotter. Even bigger inside me.

I know it's coming. He's going to cum inside my ass. I can feel it. He pulls me close, so close. I snake my arms around him, pulling him against me. I don't want him to get away. I want to feel him. I need to feel him.

I feel him pulsing, twitching. And then... it's like there is pure heat flowing into me. It's filling me up. Where I need it most.

He groans as he cums inside my ass, and I moan with him. He stays inside me for a while, rocking against me, his cock shifting inside my ass, now so full with his warm cum. I become aware of his hand, gripping my breast painfully hard. When did it get there? I wonder dreamily.

Now that he's finished, I feel... used. I feel his.

Now he's done with me, he lets me sink to the floor, his cock sliding out, still so hard. I can feel his cum trickling down my leg.

"Did you like that?" He asks above me.

"Yes, sir. I love it when you cum in my ass," I say, breathless.

"Good girl," he says, and strokes my hair a little bit more. He's still hard. He's still twitching. Right in front of my face.

"Spread your ass again for me, pet," he says, and I do it for him, right there on the floor. He takes a picture of my ass, full of his cum. I feel so dirty. I feel so good.

"Now, get up. Take off my clothes," he says.

I smile. "Yes, sir," I say, and bounce to my feet. I like taking off his clothes for him.

Master is really tall. Even standing, I only reach up to his chest. I start unbuttoning his shirt, one button at a time, revealing the pale skin beneath. It feels like I'm unwrapping a birthday present.

He pets me while I'm busy working the buttons. He strokes my hair, sliding his fingers through the curls, playing with it. I glance up at him a few times, and our eyes catch.

As my body calms down from the pounding he gave me, I start feeling a kind of wonderful, warm emptiness in my ass. It's really nice.

"Thank you for using my ass, sir," I tell him.

He lifts up my face up to him. Then he brings his lips down to mine and kisses me. His mouth tastes salty and sweet.

"You're welcome, pet," he says finally. "How should I use you next?" he asks.

I bite my lip. Anywhere is fine. He could fuck my ass again. He could use my cunt and stop me from Cumming. But he likes straight answers.

"My mouth, sir," I say.

He smiles. "Good answer," he says, and kisses me again.

I smile back. I'm done with his shirt now. He lets me slide it off his body.

"Now, my pants and boxers too," he says.

I get down on my knees and tug off his pants and boxers. He steps out of them for me. And now he's totally, gloriously naked.

Still on my knees, I notice there is a bead of cum glistening at the tip of his cock. And I want it in my mouth.

"May I clean your cock, sir?" I ask.

He smiles down at me. "What, you don't care I just fucked your ass?"

I whimper a bit when he says it. I can still feel his cum on my thighs.

"I... it... I like it, sir," I manage.

"You are such a dirty slut, you know that?"

"Thank you, sir!" I say.

He nods. "Alright. Hands beh—"

But I've already put them behind my back, clasping them firmly.

He chuckles. "Good girl," he says, pleased with my eagerness. "You're being such a good girl today. You haven't disappointed me once."

"Yes, sir," I smile. "I... I try hard."

He smiles.

I kiss the tip of his cock, sucking the drop of cum into my mouth. I lick my lips, and he laughs.

"Do you like how it tastes?" he asks.

I smile up at him. "Yes, sir. I love it." I lick my lips again, and he strokes my hair.

First, I lick him all over, making him wet and shiny with my spit. Then I wrap my lips around the head and suck hard, my lips squeezing every last drop of cum out of him.

"God, I forgot what a greedy little mouth you had," he says. He gets his phone again, and points the camera at me.

"Smile for the camera, pet," he says, and I do, his cock still hard and twitching in my mouth. I even make a V sign at the camera.

He laughs. "Perfect. I'll make it my desktop background at work," he says, and I chuckle, with him still in my mouth.

"I'm going to use your mouth now, pet," he says.

"Yes, sir,"

"Good girl. Now, open," he says, and lightly smacks my cheek.

I open my mouth wide for him, on command, and stick my tongue under his twitching cock. I look up into his eyes.

"Are you ready?" He asks.

"Mhm," I nod. I'm ready.

And then I can feel him. Pushing his cock into my mouth. Deeper. Deeper. His cock slides into my throat like it was nothing. Like it was made for him. He's so long. He's so thick. I can't breathe. I can't speak. I clench my hands tight behind my back, refusing to disappoint him.

He pushes himself even deeper. God. My mouth is so full of him. And then... my lips are touching the base of his cock. My eyes are closed. I feel so strangely proud of myself, that I could take everything. All of him.

I hear him groaning above me. He thrusts himself once into my throat.

And then he pulls out, and finally, I take a deep breathe.

"Good girl," he says above me.

"Again, please," I say, and open my mouth for him, looking up into his eyes again.

He shoves his cock into my mouth again. Down my throat. He holds me down, strong hands not letting my surface, not letting me breathe. He slides out, and then slides in again. Again. And again. Fucking my mouth. Using my throat. He groans with every thrust; a raw, feral sound that touches something inside me.

And then, just when I think I can't take it anymore, just when I realize I have to take a breath, he pulls out with another one of his deep groans. His cock is covered in my spit. It's twitching right in front of my eyes.

I try to catch my breath. But I want him in my mouth again. So much.

I take him in my mouth again, without his hands this time. My eyes locked on his, I let him slide deeper, deeper. Deeper. I push him down my throat. I swallow around him. He's so big. He moans.

I move my mouth back and forth around him, letting him slide in and out of my throat. His hands are on my head now, but no longer pushing me. But he's still thrusting his hips a little, unable to control them. I cup his balls in my hand and feel them, stroke them.

And suddenly his hands are on me again. He doesn't warn me this time. He just grabs my head and pushes himself into my throat, his cock cutting off my moan. He holds me down and thrusts. My hands strain behind my back. But I'm a good girl. And I love it when he uses me however, he likes.

He lets go of me again. I catch my breath, and then take his cock into my mouth, again in control. I let him slide in and out of my throat. I swallow around him. I let my tongue move the little it can, stroking him. And I feel him getting harder again. Hotter.

"Oh god, oh, Jane— oh my god," he moans.

God yes. Yes. I want to taste you. I want to swallow you. Cum for me.

I let him slide out, keeping just the tip of him in my mouth, because he likes to cum into my mouth that way.

"Oh my god," he moans again. He cups my face in his hands. He strokes my hair. Gentle now.

His whole body seems to tense up, right before it happens. His legs shake. His face goes a little funny. And then he moans again. His cock pulses between my lips, almost escaping from my mouth. I have to take it in my hand to stop it, but I don't care. I want to taste him. I want to drink him.

Jets of hot cum stream into my mouth as he trembles over me. As he moans over me. They try to slide right down into my throat, but I don't let them. I want to keep his cum in my mouth. I want to taste him. I want to show him what a dirty slut I am. What a good girl I am.

He's in a different world now. I feel so proud of myself. I smile broadly as his cum streams into my mouth. As his cock pulsates and his body shakes, his hands gentle on my head.

And then, finally, but far too soon, it's over. He's shivering above me, like he just came in from the cold. Maybe that's how the weather is in orgasm-land right now. But I like watching him wind-down too. And I like the feeling of him going softer in my mouth. I squeeze him and suck the last drops of cum out, as he moans shakily, so sensitive now. So vulnerable.

Sucking master's cock always gives me a power trip. I don't know why. Maybe it's because of how gentle he gets in the end. Or maybe it's watching his face go funny.

I play with his cum in my mouth a little, tasting it. It doesn't taste like much. No, it's not the food of the gods. But I like it anyway. It's his, after all.

"Do you want to see?" I manage, with my mouth full, because I want to swallow already.

"See?" He asks, confused. Yup. He's not all there yet.

Still smiling, I open my mouth and show him.

"Oh god," he whispers. "You look so fucking hot."

"Picture!" I yell to him.

"Oh, right," he says. He grabs his phone and points the camera at me. I smile, with his load thick and white in my mouth.

"Can I swallow?" I ask.

"Yeah," he says softly.

He watches me as I take his cum down with one gulp. I open my now-empty mouth.

"How was it?" he asks, a smile on his face.

"Hmm. I want more. Gimme." He laughs.

"Fine then," I say. "I'll have to take it by force."

I take his softening cock in my mouth again.

"A-ow, ow!" he yells, laughing. But I don't care. I just suck him dry, to the last drop.

"God, Jane, that last orgasm. That was fucking amazing. How do you do that?"

I laugh. "I guess I'm just good at sucking cock," I say, happiness bubbling out of me. I feel drunk. I feel like I just took on the world... and won. I feel so good. Like I can do anything.

I stand up and pull his face to mine. We kiss for a long time. But I can't keep my smile down, and it keeps interrupting.

But really, there's something I have to ask him. "So, what are you going to do with the pictures?"

"What, you don't think getting into the porn business is a good idea?"

"Very funny," I say with a smile.

"I'm sure the faculty won't mind. And your students will certainly see a different side of you."

I laugh. "Don't even say that word right now. P—"

His hand. Between my legs. I yelp.

"You were saying?"

I moan in response. I stiffen. I put my hand in his arm. I want him to move it.

And he does move. So very slowly. His fingers scraping my pussy. I tremble.

"Did you really think we were done? You haven't even cum once yet," he whispers to me.

"P-Please, sir," I say, pleading.

"Ah, so it's back to 'sir' now, is it?" He asks with an evil smile.

"I—I'm... sorry. Please. Please."

His smile slowly fades. There's something else on his face now. Not amusement.

"Please, sir. I—"I jump. His fingers slide inside me. Just a little.

He kisses my neck. I can feel his teeth sinking into the skin. His fingers slide deeper. I moan.

"How do you do that?" He whispers into my ear. He's getting hard again. I can feel him against my stomach.

"Do what, sir?" I ask, voice shaky.

His teeth again. Hot breath. Warm, soft lips. His fingers inside me. I need him.

"Everything you do turns me on so much. I can't be around you for one second without getting hard. Again, and again."

I flush. A warm feeling spreads through my stomach, together with his praise. And I thought I was done being his. There is still so much more to have.

"Thank you, sir," I say, breathless.

He takes my collar off for me, and picks me up, his arms under my ass. I cling to him, trusting him, letting him carry me wherever he wants. To the moon for all I care. So long as he's the one doing it. So long as I can be with him.

But... he only takes me to the bedroom, not the moon. He drops me unceremoniously on the bed. Our bed is really big. Like, really big. It would have to be, wouldn't it? Considering how long we spend in it. Other people get a home cinema. We have our own form of entertainment...

I crawl back, right to the bedpost. I expect him to crawl over me, but he doesn't. Instead, he rounds the bed and grabs my hand. He pushes it against the bedpost and locks a hand-cuff into place. I bite my lip in anticipation.

"Your other hand, Jane," he says. I place it against the bedpost, my eyes locked on his face. I'm so wet.

And then it's done. I'm lying naked, spread-eagled on the bed, my legs spreading themselves for him almost unconsciously. And he's naked and gorgeous and perfect. Muscular and tall. But disappointingly, only half-hard.

My eyes are on him now. Hungry for him. I rattle the cuffs, just to make sure they're holding me in place.

He grabs the phone and takes a photo of me. I make sure to spread my legs extra wide and look straight at the camera, like the slut I am.

I realize I'm breathing hard. I'm hot all over. I'm opening and closing my legs. I'm so wet I'm staining the sheets a little.

He's hardening now. Seeing me like this. So desperate for his cock.

"Please, sir," I say. "I need your cock so much. I need you in me. Please. I need to feel you. I'm so wet."

He climbs on the bed, his cock totally hard. I spread my legs for him. His cock is so sexy above me, between my legs. I push my crotch up, my cunt needing him so bad.

"I haven't tasted you today, have I?" He asks.

I just moan in response.

Then he bends down, his face looking so hot between my legs. He licks my cunt. Just one lick. But it sends electricity through me. Another one. I'm shaking. I'm so on edge. After he came in my ass and in my mouth.

"Please, please, sir—"he gives me another lick. "Sir, I can't—"another lick. "Please, sir, I'm going to cum."

"You're not allowed to cum, pet." he says.

"I-I'm sorry sir, I can't—"another lick "I can't—can't stop myself. I don't want to disappoint you."

He looks up then, smiling. "Really?"

"Y-Yes, sir," I say, trying to catch my breath.

"Don't you want to cum?"

"I'm your property, sir. I only cum when you tell me to."

"Good girl. Very good girl."

I smile wide, happy I pleased him.

"I think, for that, you deserve a special reward," he says.

"A specia—"I yelp. His tongue again. But lower. I bite my lip.

He laughs. He gives my asshole another playful lick, and I make a small, surprised sound, like a squeal. He laughs again.

And then he starts licking my ass in earnest. It feels... so nice... like... he's scratching an itch I never even knew I had. But in a really, really, delightfully soft way. It's a soothing balm for my sore little asshole.

"I love that sound you make," he says softly.

"Wha—"I squeal when his tongue slides inside me, just the tip.

"That sound," he says.

I just moan and move my hips a little. This is really good. Why have we never done this before?

And then he starts stroking my cunt too.

Oh my god.

"Sir—I—"I begin.

"You can cum, pet," he says. His tongue is still busy at my asshole, making me feel... wonderful. And his fingers... are sliding inside me. My legs spread wider.

"Oh god, sir, oh god. Don't stop. Please. Please. Pl—" but I have to moan again. And then I can't speak. Because it feels so good. And now his fingers are inside my cunt. And I can feel his tongue in my ass. And—Oh god. Oh god. My lower body keeps bucking, as though trying to get away. But I can't escape his tongue. Or his fingers. And anyway, I'm cuffed to the bed.

He touches my clit then—

I scream when I cum. There is lightning and an all-consuming burst of pleasure. There is heat. There is no time. There is no sight. There is no sound. Just the glorious feeling of the man I love with his tongue up my butt.

Frat Party

It was my first big party of the year. I had come with my friend Amanda. Being from a small college in a small town, we often made the drive to the nearest state school, where there was always a party or two on the weekend, especially at the frat houses. Soon after arriving, however, Amanda ran into a group of friends from back home. She hadn't seen them in a while and had lots of catching up, and since I wasn't into standing around listening to other people's conversations, I moved on. So now I was cruising the house by myself, looking for something interesting. I'm not a real beer fan, but at a frat party, that's pretty much the thing to do, and after two quick ones, I was feeling good - just barely tipsy. On my third trip back to the keg, I found two girls "standing guard" (their term). "Beer patrol!" the one yelled. Oh brother, I thought, these two are blasted already.

"I'm Amy and this is Carmella," the one said, very pseudo-officially, "You must answer all our questions if you want a beer." She then proceeded to ask a series of totally inane questions about school, music, drinking, guys, and, of course, sex. Alright, I thought,

Ill play along. Actually, they were both pretty cute, so what the hell - good things could always happen. During the sex questions, I made sure they knew I was bisexual and available, just in case.

"Final question," Amy said. "Name?"

"Milene," I answered.

"Oooo, interesting name," Amy said. "For that, you get an extra beer." Her friend, however, looked perplexed. "Milene? Why do I know that name?" As Amy rambled on, Carmella kept looking at me and talking to herself, trying to remember some connection she might have with me while I continued talking to her friend Amy.

Finally it hit her: "Oh....Milene??? Milene! Omigod! I know who you are! Yes! Yessss! You're that lez chick, right? Right???"

Her friend went wide-eyed at the question. "Carmella!!!!"

For my part, I took the question in stride. It wasn't the first time. "Well, yeah," I responded, "I like girls, I told you that." I acted indifferent, but inside, my guts were churning. "But what exactly do you mean by 'that lez chick'?"

"You're the one they always talk about - the one that ate out a bunch of girls at a frat party a couple years ago - everybody's heard that story." Carmella looked at Amy, who nodded knowingly. "And," she continued, this time to Amy, "she still comes to frat parties, hoping to pick up girls."

Wow. They really did know about me. And apparently a lot of others did, too. Off guard, I stammered a response. "Uummmmm, well, stories like that really get exaggerated, you know?" God, it sounded so pathetic.

It was true - it had been exaggerated. It was only two girls, not "a bunch", and I was drunk as hell - the dangers of drinking too much too young. Still, it was at a frat party, one of the first my freshman year, and it had pretty well set my reputation ever since. But it wasn't all bad. It did tend to start conversations - as evidenced by the situation at hand.

"Wow, I assumed you were just an urban legend."

"Hey look, I'm just a girl," I shrugged, "just like you." I feigned indifference, but I was uncomfortable with the conversation. At the same time, however, my mind was racing, considering the possibilities. I searched Carmella's face for clues. Was she curious, disgusted ... interested?

"Speak for yourself, chickie!" Amy protested. "I've definitely never eaten anyone out! Especially in front of a bunch of guys."

"Yeah, babe" Carmella chimed in slyly, "but you know you ARE an amazing kisser. I think the rest of us are probably missing out on a good thing." She punctuated the last comment with a tongue motion that made her implication very clear. Amy responded with a push and an only half-serious glare.

There was a short pause among the three of us, one of those dreaded lulls, which gave me a chance to check them out a little better. They were both "preppy" types - Polos and shorts - and both about six inches taller than me - around five-eight. Amy had a typical WASP look: straight, dirty-blonde hair down to her shoulders, and somewhat thin nose, and grey-green eyes. She had slim, "boyish" hips, but on top she was all girl - her pink polo was just tight enough to show off a nice pair of breasts. And from what I could see, she had sweet little butt. Carmella, on the other hand, was well-tanned, with a slightly Latino look to her. She was athletic, though not buff, and her breasts were hard to ignore, full and firm. Her short, black hair was subtlety spiked, and she had a cute button nose over dark eyes that exuded self confidence. Beyond all that, she had a voice that gave me chills - low and breathy, it sounded like sex. I let my mind wander a bit - thinking of what it would be like to be with these two girls, when Carmella suddenly took a big swig of beer, cocked one eyebrow, and started up again.

"Sooooooo..." she paused, swaying back and forth seductively, "I guess you're, uh... looking for pussy tonight, huh?" Carmella tried to say serious, but couldn't suppress a grin. More like a smirk, really. Whether she was mocking me or just playing along, I couldn't tell. Amy's jaw simply dropped, before she stifled a giggle of her own.

It took me a second to react myself. I felt a familiar tingle inside as I realized that this could be leading somewhere very good. Feeling cocky, I looked her straight in the eye and, using my sweetest voice and my best "bedroom look", purred, "Oh, I'm always looking for new pussy, baby. That's what I do ...I eat pussy....and give orgasms." I smiled knowingly and looked her up and down, pausing intently on her pelvic area before continuing. "So is there some particular sweet pussy you think I might get tonight?"

My boldness caught her off guard. Carmella glanced nervously at her friend. She was clearly moving down a new path for her, while Amy just stepped back a bit, staring at her friend with a "what are you doing????" look on her face.

Finally, Carmella regained her cool confidence and responded, rather nonchalantly, "Well, I guess that depends. Are you any good?"

"You mean with my mouth?" I asked. I was trying to draw the conversation out, being suggestive, letting her go where I hoped she wanted to. She barely nodded, and I continued playing into their rumors. Looking pointedly into her eyes, I cooed softly, "Why, haven't you heard, baby? I'm the best. They say you're never the same once you get head from Milene. I'll totally spoil you." Now it was my turn to smirk.

I couldn't believe I was being this aggressive. Must be the alcohol again, I thought. Plus the fact that I'd been celibate for almost a month. In any case, I could tell that Carmella was right on the edge, playing this as a big tease but with some genuine interest under the surface, not ruling out a little adventure. Emboldened by the drinks and becoming increasingly aroused, I kept pushing forward. I leaned into Carmella and let my hand graze lightly up the back of her thigh as I whispered in her ear: "Just make sure you have some extra sheets, sweetie - 'cuz you're gonna leave a HUGE wet spot on the bed when I do you." Damn, just saying that to her turned me on something fierce.

Carmella stared at me for a long moment, startled by my boldness, unsure how to respond. There was an almost imperceptible change in her breathing. I knew then that I was having an effect on her.

I leaned in again and said, just for her to hear "My tongue will take you places you've never been before. Seriously. And it will go anyplace you want it."

Reaching back to squeeze one cheek of her cute bottom, I whispered again for emphasis, "Anyplace!" then swirled my tongue sensuously around her ear. She shivered, and her eyes got REALLY big, but there was no hiding her pleasure and, I hoped, anticipation.

After a few moments, she gathered herself enough to respond: "Well, that's something to think about, isn't it?" She was back to be cool and collected. I loved this girl. Amy remained silent, letting Carmella take the lead.

Letting the topic rest for a while, we made small talk and drank some more. I sipped mine, hoping to remain in control of my senses, to leave as many options open as possible. Amy and Carmella, meanwhile, just kept going. They were either serious drinkers or they were nervous with the situation.

I eventually decided it was time to make a move. "So what's the story, ladies?" I said lightly, trying my best not to be pushy or threatening. "Are you up for a little adventure, or do you want to stay at this lame party all night?"

They looked at each other, obviously unsure. Luckily, the alcohol seemed to be having it's usual effect, and they were at least considering it. They whispered a brief discussion, seemed to argue just a little, and then Carmella asked "So which one? Who are you really asking? And what do you expect from us?"

Wow, I thought, this might really happen. "Both of you," I said. I smiled sweetly and added, "How could I choose?"

"Both?" Carmella exclaimed, doing her best to keep her voice down. "You want to do both of us, together?"

"Sure," I said, "that's half the fun. Haven't you ever watched someone else have sex? Or wanted to?"

Amy quickly interrupted. "Hey, I ain't eatin' nobody's pussy, I'll tell you right now. You two can do whatever, but I'm no lesbo."

I hate that term, but I managed to hide my distaste for her language and tried to soothe her. "You don't have to do anything, hon, really. If you want to that's cool, but if not, you guys are both really cute, and I'll be perfectly happy to do all the 'eating' - for both of you."

Then, looking them both in the eye, I added, "And trust me, you won't believe how good it can be. It's not like with a guy. I'll stretch it out and make you cum over and over and over, better than you've ever had."

They conferred again briefly, and then my heart fluttered as Carmella said, "Okay, we can go to our place. It's pretty close."

I followed them to Carmella's car, admiring both of their sweet buns from behind - very, very nice. Damn, I thought, I must be really horny. I always get obsessed with girls' tushies when I'm horny. I asked them to drive me to my car - I wanted to make sure they didn't change their minds and ditch me. I could already feel the moisture in my panties as I thought about what I'd soon be doing. I couldn't believe I was going to get to play with these two.

As I followed them to their place, I watched their interaction in the car, trying to interpret what they were saying. I could tell that Amy was still very unsure about the whole deal. Interpreting their gestures and body language from behind, it seemed like Amy was questioning why Carmella wanted to do this. On the other hand, Carmella seemed to argue that it would be fun, an adventure. I was sure that Amy had never been with a girl before. As for Carmella, I wasn't sure, but she was definitely into it now. Even if Amy backed out - a distinct possibility - doing Carmella alone would be a delight.

When we got to their apartment there was another of those awkward moments. There we were, and we all agreed why, but no one knew how to start. We drank a little more and then I figured it was up to me, so I spoke up. "So you're a good kisser, huh, Amy?"

Amy flushed deeply and I thought I'd made a mistake. She was the reluctant one, after all. But Carmella came to the rescue, chiming in with "Oh yeah, she's a hot one. This girl's got a tongue. We made out on a dare one night at a party and I thought I was gonna wet my pants!"

"I think you did wet your pants," Amy retorted. "You know you've always been hot for me." They both broke into laughter and the ice was broken.

"Okay, so let's see," I teased. "Let's see if you can get her hot, Amy." Emboldened by the talk and the beer, Amy took the challenge, grabbing Carmella and giving her a long, passionate kiss, with lots of tongue and roving hands. By the time the broke apart, both girls were flushed (and not from embarrassment) and I was way hot myself. "Don't I get any of that?" I pouted.

Amy obliged, and she didn't disappoint. She was indeed a great kisser, with soft, active lips that traced seductively over my own and a swirling tongue that explored all the right places in my mouth. I ran my hands up and down her body, finally settling on that darling butt of hers, becoming more and more aroused as I felt her up. I slipped my hand down the back of her pants and let my fingers explore briefly between her cheeks. Damn, I was horny now! When she finally pulled away, Amy's breath was short and her nostrils flared, and I knew I was in for an incredible night. It wouldn't be just Carmella and I.

Carmella came next, and if anything, she was better. Her kisses weren't as soft and sweet as Amy's, but they were hotter, filled with urgent passion. This time it was her hands that were roaming, exploring me. And her tongue, oh my god, that girl's tongue was just nasty. Soft and wet, slow and erotic, her tongue kissing made me weak in the knees. I could feel the dampness building between my legs.

"Okay," I said, almost desperate now to have one of them, "who's going to do this?"

"Well, sweetie," Carmella teased, "I think YOU'RE going to do it. The question is, 'who are you going to do?'"

After some brief discussion, they decide that Carmella would go first. Amy wasn't so sure, anyway, and the whole thing had been Carmella's idea. "Besides," she whispered just for me to hear, "I'm really, really horny." THAT really got me going. We started in on one another again, groping, frenching, until we were both moaning with need. I pulled her shirt out of her shorts and, taking the hint, she quickly pulled it over her head, revealing a white lacy bra that held those luscious tits I'd been admiring earlier. Next came the shorts. She took her time, clearly wanting to tease me with her body, getting off on the idea of turning on the famous Milene. When her bra came off, I almost gasped as she revealed two beautiful breasts, topped with large, dark areolas stippled with tiny bumps. I've never really been a "tit girl", but big nipples always get to me. I wanted to pounce on her right there and just suck like a baby.

My reaction must have been obvious. "Well, well, you like these, don't you?" Carmella noted, taunting me playfully and holding her prizes up for a better view. Then, in a very coquettish voice that just made me shiver, "You wanna suck 'em?"

Jesus, did I ever! But I stayed cool despite myself. "All in good time, hon. We have all night."

I told her to leave her panties on for now. I wanted to do that myself - always a thrill the first time. I moved into her and took another kiss, a short one, followed by a long, lusty one that went on for minutes. I let my hands enjoy her breasts, cupping them, caressing them, tweaking the nipples between my thumb and forefinger. Damn, this was good! Unable to resist any longer, I kissed my way down her neck, to her shoulder, and then captured one large, delicious nipple in my mouth. I licked at the bumpy surface, sucked gently on the rubbery nipple, and used my tongue to trap it against the roof of my mouth. Carmella's head dropped back, her eyes closed, a rapturous look on her face as I suckled, going back and forth between her magnificent soft mounds.

I sucked her tits for a long time, slowly building her arousal. I extended my tongue and ran it slowly along the crease under each of Carmella's breasts, at the same time keeping my fingers busy, kneading the thick buds of her nipples, pinching them, lightly twisting them. My lips moved up and around her breasts, encircling her excited nipples without touching them, doing my best to drive her crazy. Carmella was loving it, murmuring "Mmmmmm, yeah, mmmmm" over and over.

Finally I urged her to her left, over to the bed, and sat her down on the edge. Kneeling before her, I reached up and worked my fingers into the elastic band of the white bikinis. I looked up and gave her a smile that hinted of all the treats to come. God, I was so grateful for this opportunity. I slowly pulled her panties down as Carmella raised her hips slightly to assist. As soon as they were off, she spread her legs wide. She was ready for me.

Carmella had a beautiful cunt, a glistening, scarlet juice pit, framed by fleshy, succulent lips that just begged to be sucked. A small v-shaped patch of dark hair just above served as an accent, pointing down to her opening and, in particular to a rather large, engorged clitoris. I imagined how that firm little nub would feel in my mouth. I looked up and she was watching me, watching me survey her honeypot, apparently looking for a reaction. I looked her straight in the eyes and whispered "Nice, it's beautiful," and she grinned smugly, apparently very satisfied to hear that I liked her pussy.

Keeping my eyes on hers, I leaned to the right to kiss, then slowly lick at her inner thigh. That drew a just little smile, but then, as I licked in tiny circles upward, she sighed and trembled slightly. Her thighs spread just a bit wider, hoping for more. Her hands began to softly stroke the outsides of her thighs as I continued to work the inner surfaces, and her hips began an easy, barely perceptible up and down motion.

"You ready?", I asked. I knew she was. Though her facial expression was still fairly calm and detached, her movements, her breathing, and her aroma all revealed her state of arousal.

With an audible "Mmmm", Carmella raised her knees, resting her feet on the edge of the bed. I glanced over at Amy to see her reaction. Her breathing was heavy now, her stare focused, like mine, on that sweet spot between Carmella's legs. I smiled briefly at her, making it clear that I knew she was watching, as I eased my face into Carmella's wet trough. As I did, Carmella dropped her head back and uttered a gentle "Ahhhhhhh."

The initial wetness was amazing - the flowing stream almost overwhelming. The lengthy build-up had caused her faucet to flow, and the cunt syrup was everywhere. I was only boasting earlier about making a wet spot, but I could see now that it would certainly be true. Already her fluids were seeping out of her, running down between the cheeks of her ass. I licked her slowly, gathering the nectar, avoiding her clitoris except for an occasional rub with the tip of my nose. My mouth and chin were inundated with her warm juices. Now my tongue probed more deeply, my mouth pressing against the opening as I held the fleshy lips to each side with my fingers. Unable to hold back now, Carmella groaned and started rocking toward me as my tongue danced in her vagina. She leaned back slightly, supporting her upper body on her hands and forearms, pushing her lower portions up into my mouth.

It was oddly quiet. The room was silent except for the continual moans from Carmella's throat and the liquid clicking sounds made by my tongue and lips as I sucked at her cunt. I kept it slow, aiming for a gradual, growing stimulation, which I knew would result, over time, in an intensely satisfying orgasm. Not yet though. I was determined to make this last a long time, to assure we both enjoyed it to the maximum degree. Over and over, I kissed her lips and the sensitive parts inside, occasionally sucking the tender flesh into my mouth or moving up briefly to tease her now needy clit with my tongue. Her hips thrust more urgently upward and her groans became louder, more guttural. Alternating with quieter, whimpering sounds, they revealed the intensity of her growing need.

By this time, Carmella had dropped all pretense of being detached and was in full pursuit of her orgasm. Using her hands, she pulled her knees all the way back and drew her legs wide apart. I felt faint with excitement as she opened herself up for me, losing all her inhibitions, focused completely on the pleasures I was giving her. Taking her cue, I held her knees back, opening her up even more and diving in face first. Her hands grabbed my head, twisting in my hair, jamming my mouth farther up inside her, creaming my face. I adored the wetness. The wetness was an affirmation of my ability to please her. I scoured her hole, cleaning it, sucking at it. I tried again to avoid her clitoris, but it was just too tempting, protruding now from its hood, straining for more attention. I took it into my mouth and briefly played with it, rolling my tongue over its tender surface as Carmella cried and squealed above me.

Not yet, I thought. You're not ready for it yet. It's going to get much, much better, girl, better than you ever imagined it could be. I pulled my mouth away from her and looked lower, down between the cheeks of her ass. Her perfect brown ring was wet and shiny from the juices that had oozed out of her cunt and dribbled down to it. My tongue moved forward again, scooping up her girl-juice and tickling her butthole. A little squeal of surprise escaped her lips at that first touch, followed by soft keening sounds and then, "Ohhhhhhh God, fuck! Oh god, yeah!" Her hips rose shamelessly off the bed to give me better access. I let my tongue wander several times around the little muscle. Carmella sighed and whimpered pathetically, all inhibition gone now, feeling nothing but the delicious slithering sensation of my tongue on her most private place. Heavenly.

As I began to eat Carmella's ass in earnest, I glanced over at Amy. She was quite flushed now, her eyes huge, fixed on the erotic sight before her, of her roommate having her pussy, and now her ass, eaten by this strange girl. She too had dropped all pretense of propriety and had her right hand busy in the crotch of her shorts. Mmmmmm, I thought, a good sign there.

I continued to kiss and lick Carmella's asshole for some time, occasionally tickling the center with my tongue tip, even nudging a bit inside. Eventually I moved back up, running the flat of my tongue ever so slowly up inside her, from the base of her slit to her hood and back again, several times. Gobs of cunt cream entered my mouth. My god, she was leaking everywhere. She was trembling now, so close, her thighs moving back and forth as the room filled with her pathetic moans. I was trembling, too, so excited. It was time, for both of us, and my lips captured her meaty little clit, sucking in a rhythm to match her own thrusts. Just for good measure, I slipped a finger underneath her and into her well-lubricated bottom.

That did it. Carmella grabbed my head again, forcing my mouth roughly up and down within her greasy crevice. She let out a sharp cry, another "OMIGOD!" and then just lost it. Her hips bucked frantically back and forth. Her back arched more than I thought possible, then both actions were repeated with even greater fervor, accompanied by short cries of ecstasy. The jerking action wiped her puss back and forth across my face, soaking me from nose to chin with her wet heat. I jammed my finger all the way up her ass, did my best to hold on, and drank from the fountain.

After what seemed like minutes but was probably only 20 - 30 seconds, she finally started to come down. After-tremors shook her body, little hip twitches that came and went every few seconds. I could feel the muscles inside her anus clenching spasmodically around my finger. I kept licking, gently lapping up her juice until she finally pushed me away. "No more," she pleaded, still panting desperately, "please ...too much."

Reluctantly, I eased my finger out of her rear, gave her sweet pussy one last kiss, and let her be.

I looked up at her inquisitively. "Well?" I asked. Carmella just nodded, acknowledging that I had been as good as promised. Between breaths, she murmured "Damn" a few times, smiling with satisfaction.

I looked over at Amy inquisitively. "Well??" I asked. She said nothing at first. She was still staring at the bed, obviously thinking about the monster, mind-numbing orgasm that Carmella had just had. The she eagerly nodded her head and came over to join me on the bed.

I quickly wiped Carmella's cunt slime off my face and, grabbing Amy by the ears, kissed her passionately. Her startled reaction intensified when she realized she was tasting her best friend's pussy on my tongue, but she got over that quickly and we settled in for a quick little make-out session. By the time we came up for air, she was ready for more.

"Get out of these clothes!" I exclaimed, and she quickly stripped down to nothing. I did the same - even if this was to be all one-sided, I knew I would at least have to play with myself while I munched on them.

Naked, Amy was a cutie, a peaches and cream type. As her bra came off, I saw that her breasts were slightly smaller than Carmella's, but nicely shaped, with pretty pink nipples that, I noted, were already erect. She turned around When she lowered her shorts, I assume to hide her pubic area. I had to chuckle - odd time to be modest, and I was about to do much more than look! Her shorts and panties came down in one motion, revealing the crack and then the entirety of her backside, Damn, she did have a nice ass, perfect round globes with just enough "overhang", separated by a fairly wide crease that just begged for attention. I knew Amy would be less adventuresome than Carmella, but I promised myself that I would explore that perfect bottom before we were done. Given Amy's current state of arousal and what I was about to do for her, I was confident that I'd get the chance.

We started kissing again, but I could tell that neither of us were interested in many preliminaries. We fell down on the bed (which Carmella had thoughtfully vacated) and my right hand dove immediately between her legs.

I teased her a bit, my fingertips playing lightly with her lips, just on the outside I slipped my middle fingertip into her slit, just inside and felt the warm gush of fluid that I knew would be there. Amy groaned quietly and pushed her pelvis up to me. Impatient myself, I slowly pushed one long finger into her hot, greasy channel. God, it felt so good in there! I slipped another in beside it and moved them back and forth in a scissors motion. Amy's fingers dug into my shoulders and her mouth got more insistent on my own. I pushed a third finger inside and began moving them in and out as her cunny gripped them hard. I pulled out of her and made a show of licking one finger clean, then offered the others to her. Amy licked her own juices from my fingers like she was one of the "lesbos" she talked about. I grinned in satisfaction and anticipation of things to come.

Knowing she was ready, I began my trek down Amy's body, pausing briefly at her tits, but quickly moving down over hr ribcage to her soft, taut belly. I tongue-tickled her navel a bit, then ran my wet tongue farther down, over her hip bones, closer and closer to her "vee", but not quite where I knew she wanted me. She was squirming around, trying her best to get me into her pleasure pit, when I finally positioned myself strategically between her now wide-open thighs, her dripping snatch right before my eyes.

Amy had a "pretty" pussy, a rather small, pink slit that just peeked out from between her legs. The outer lips were puffy and the inner ones smaller and more demure than Carmella's, though definitely beautiful in their own way. They were clearly engorged now, and I could see a hint of the moisture inside.

I leaned forward and placed a very chaste kiss (if that's really possible) at the center of her pussy. Just a peck to get her started. Even still, I came away with a bit of her on my lips, which I quickly licked off. She tasted good. I knew she would. I went back in for more, this time using my tongue, french-kissing her juicy slot, then running it slowly up one side and down the other. Her legs spread even wider and a long, low moan filled the room. "Pleeeease," she begged. "Come on...please."

How could I resist? I dove in like a madwoman, feverishly eating her out, using every technique I knew to raise her passion higher and higher but not let her get over the top. Carmella had had her gut-wrenching orgasm, so why should Amy get anything less?

As I continued my Amy-meal, I could tell that her barriers were coming down. The pleasure I was giving her was intense, so intense that all other thoughts, all previous "rules" were driven out of her mind. I knew it was time to take what I wanted. Still licking her twat, I slowly inched down, stroking her perineum, then lower, letting my tongue glance over the top edge of Amy's anus.

I felt her body twitch and heard a little cry of surprise, and, I hoped, delight. I went back to it, this time swiping a couple times over the entire hole, then circling it, spiraling inward.

"Oh, unnnnghhhhhhggg, God, mmmmmmmmmehh!"

"You like that?" I asked, though the answer was clear.

"Yesssss. Fuck!!! No one's ever done that to me before."

Mmmmm, I always love being a first for someone, and now I was at least a double first for Amy. I proceeded to lick oh so slowly all-around Amy's pretty pink asshole and was rewarded with a wonderfully agonized groan of pleasure from my newly perverted sex kitten. "Unnnnghhhhh...mmmmmm...ahhhhh. God! More! please...don't stop... Pleeeeaassse!"

None of this was lost on Carmella, who was watching intently from her chair. "Damn, girl, you're something else." I looked over and promised, "You're next". She was playing with herself as she watched, but she didn't stop when I spoke to her. All self-control and shame were gone at this point. Hedonism had taken over all of us.

I turned Amy over onto her stomach and pulled her up slightly onto her knees. Her face was buried in a pillow as she lewdly offered her beautiful bottom to me. I ran my tongue slowly up and down the crack of her ass several times, pausing each time to give special attention to her overly-stimulated anus. I was worshiping her ass now and she was loving it. Her toes curled and her hands frantically gripped the sheets. I could hear the wonderful whimpering sounds she was making into the pillow.

I went on for several minutes like that, licking her crack, biting her cheeks, and kissing and sucking at her butthole until she was out of her mind. Then I dipped further down, down to Amy's girl parts, and buried my face in her cunny. I sucked it in like a sweet piece of fruit and then ran my tongue wetly over her lips. Amy responded with ardor - a long, desperate moan - as her hips did a sexy hula-style movement against my lips. I could feel her fluids dripping freely into my mouth as I pushed my tongue as far up inside her as I could.

At this point I couldn't take it anymore. I slipped my hand between my own legs and began to satisfy myself while I continued working on Amy. I'm sure Carmella could see me, but I didn't care. In fact, I wanted her to see, to know how much I was enjoying eating Amy out. I'm sure it was no surprise anyway.

Then suddenly I felt some motion behind me, and then warm breath on my private parts. Carmella! I moved my own hand and in moments felt the wonderful flutter of a delicate female tongue exploring me from below. I moaned long and hard into Amy's soft wet folds and got back to my own task. With both hands free now, I grabbed onto Amy's hips and began hungrily gobbling her wet slit. The room soon filled with our cries of passion. Even Carmella was moaning loudly, clearly aroused by the feel of my cooze as I ground it down into her mouth.

After all that went before, there was no way I could take this for long, and in minutes I was cumming, pushing down onto Carmella's face to maintain the wonderful sensations she was giving me. Even in the throws of orgasm, I managed to keep my mouth firmly latched onto Amy's hot little cleft, sucking her luscious pink crease until she, too, was off. Her butt shook and jerked back onto my face for long, long seconds as I took in all the girl-juice she had to give. By the time it was over, we were all lying in a pile on the bed, still breathing hard, wondering what hit us. "Damn," Carmella finally panted, "that was hot! Amazing hot!" and all three of us burst into giggles.

We took a short break, but we were all still horny as hell, so it didn't last long. Lying on the bed together, it was just too easy to reach over and stroke a thigh or sneak a peak between someone's legs, and then someone would get started again. We had left the party fairly early, so we had many hours to try new variations or just repeat the earlier ones. Amy kept to her word about "not eatin' nobody's pussy" (though Carmella tried her best to get her to), and most of the activity was oral from me, but that was just fine, thank you.

I must say that my obsession her both their bums continued throughout the night. I guess I was in that mood, and it seemed to be a new thrill for both of them, because we kept falling into it. At one point, I had them side by side on the bed, face down, and was tonguing both their delectable derrieres. They made out with each other as I buried my face between first one and then the other set of soft, sexy cheeks. The kissing and fondling between them just heightened their response to my oral-anal love, and their exquisite sighs and groans made me even more eager to take their darling rosebuds in my mouth.

Once, as I pushed slowly into the deep tan circle of Carmella's anus, I heard her gasp and whisper "Oh god, she's got her whole tongue up my ass ... fuck, it's so good." That brought a cry of lust from Amy, and she kissed her friend with even more passion. I, in turn, got a shiver of excitement from hearing them respond.

I tongue-fucked Carmella's asshole with a slow, circling motion as her sweet bottom swayed back and forth for me. Then I moved away, pausing briefly to lap and suck at her sopping folds, and without missing a beat, placed my lips over the delicate ring of Amy's anus. I sucked it deeply into my mouth and she groaned loudly, thrusting her tongue down Carmella's throat as I french kissed her hot little hole.

We went on like that for a good half hour, my heart pounding wildly as I gave them both a rimming they would never forget. I was in butt-licker heaven, but of course, they wanted more than that. I had my face buried in Amy's butt for the umpteenth time when Carmella suddenly pulled me up and threw me on my back. I opened my mouth to say something, but before I could speak, I was filled with the wet heat of Carmella's cunt. She came down hard, forcing herself into my open mouth until the hot flesh of her vulva rested on the back of my tongue. I sucked at her luscious girl-flesh and felt a stream of pussy juice oozing into my throat. Her pubic hairs tickled the roof of my mouth as she force-fed me, and I was loving it. My passionate cries of delight were muffled by the slick sweetness that spread my jaws wide. I grabbed her hips with both arms and happily feasted on her until she finished.

The morning provided the usual edginess. Yes, we'd spent several hours the night before in the most intimate activities with each other, but things are always different when the sun returns and the alcohol wears off. We shared some coffee and some rather stilted conversation before I said I had to go. I think they were actually more embarrassed with each other than with me, as their friendship clearly had a different tone to it now. In any case, I did get their number, then said my goodbyes and was off. At the door, I got hugs from both, and Carmella whispered, "That really was amazing. Really good."

I took her comment as a sign of future possibilities. If not, well, there's always another frat party, isn't there?

Painting Love

A friend calls you to ask if you would be interested in doing some PR work for a charity auction. There is an internationally renowned artist donating some of his paintings, and you are interested to meet him, so you agree to take the project on.

You call the number you have been given, expecting to talk to a secretary, but he answers the 'phone himself. He has a slight Scottish accent, and sounds humorous, if somewhat laconic. You chat about the project, and agree to meet the next day at his studio.

That evening, you do your due diligence, spending your time researching him and his work. What you see is a mixture of conventional portraiture, and some exceptional abstract works, putting you in mind of Kandinsky, but not in the least derivative.

The man himself appears well dressed and smiling in his public appearances, but in the few articles where he is pictured in his studio, there is a look of intense concentration on his strong features, and his striking blue eyes are focused only on his work, seeming to ignore the camera.

You find him attractive, even though he is somewhat older. He plainly stays in shape, and you find his intensity interesting. The next morning you dress carefully, wearing a slim black skirt, and a white silk blouse.

Arriving at his studio, a large converted warehouse on the outskirts of town, you are impressed to see a black Aston Martin outside. Plainly this man is successful. You are aware his portraits are often commissioned for a great deal of money, and evidently, he is not afraid to spend his money well.

You press the entry bell, which is simply labelled with his name. He buzzes you in after a minute, and you spend the intervening period looking at the area - it is obviously an industrial zone, and the majority of the neighboring units are disused, with heavy equipment rusting in dank buildings. It's an interesting place to find a £150,000 car......

An elevator descends before you as you step into the building. The entry way is dark, but the elevator itself is well lit, one of the old steel cage types you recognize from your stays in Parisian apartments....

As the elevator clunks to a stop, the doors of the cage are opened by the artist himself. He is casually dressed in jeans and a tight black tee shirt, both of which are spattered with bright paint of different hues. He wipes his right hand on his jeans, and offers it to you.

"Welcome, I'm very pleased to meet you, and thank you for coming all the way out here. I know it's not the most salubrious of neighborhoods, but you will know why I chose it when we get upstairs."

His quick smile, slight Scottish accent, the firm pressure of his handshake, and his easy vitality put you instantly at ease. You reply that you are very much looking forward to seeing his work, and he smiles and nods "Oh, you will see plenty of my work today. I don't often admit visitors to this studio. I have what I call my 'display studio' in New York, where I keep many fewer canvases. But here is where the bulk of my work is stored, and where I really like to paint."

As he finishes speaking the elevator reaches the next floor. He pulls the gates open, and you are stunned by the amount of light that is present in what is a huge space, stretching almost 100 yards in front of you. The walls are painted a uniform bright white, and the windows are around 20 feet tall, stretching down both sides of the building. There is also a glass roof, and the floor is of some kind of light wood. The overall effect seems to amplify the morning sun that shines into the East facing windows, and the sense of space and light is powerfully affecting, after the darkness of the lobby.

He smiles, enjoying the effect that the space has on you. "I have a confession to make. The lobby downstairs was much more open too, but I deliberately enclosed it, and I keep it dimly lit, so that this space has just the effect you are experiencing now. All art is performance, and all performance is art. I bring clients here. It relaxes them. The guys I deal with are often corporate lawyers, investment bankers - those who can afford my work. I don't like discussing money with such people, I have an agent who does that. I find they are less inclined to argue prices with her once they have seen this space."

You murmur your admiration for the room, and he smiles again "why don't we step into my office, I have some tea ready." The ceiling is some 40 feet above you, and as you walk beside him towards the centre of the building, you see many canvases, some complete, others either in progress or abandoned, lining the walls.

His office consists simply of a large desk, covered in paint streaks and spatters, with a telephone and a laptop, and a silver tray, on which is a teapot and two cups. Rather than walls, the space is enclosed by large canvasses, and as he pours the tea, you examine them.

Each canvas has a scene, apparently from Africa, of children in various states of play. One shows a boy of around 6, his eyes wide as he is offered a soccer ball. Another has a girl of 10 or so, sitting cross legged with her back against a tree, intently reading a colorful picture book.

There is a luminous joy in all of the faces, which is affecting. He hands you your tea, and you ask him about the series of pictures, noting that they are nothing like his usual portrait work.

"Every artist has a project which is close to their heart," he says, ushering you to a comfortable leather sofa, and seating himself on a stool, again covered in paint splashes. "My work brings me considerable financial reward, which is nice," he says, crossing his legs, and balancing his cup on his knee. "Frankly, even if I weren't paid, I would continue to paint - that is the true definition of an artist for me - someone who has to perform their art, whether or not they are rewarded for it."

"I find the amount of money people are prepared to pay for my work frankly obscene. I have more money than I can possibly spend. I have my studio, a home in Paris, New York and Barcelona, several nice cars, and beyond that I have very few needs. I have no wife and no children. I visited Malawi a few years ago, on a photography tour of Africa, and I was struck by two things. The extreme poverty, and the extraordinary resilience, and capacity for happiness of the population - especially the children."

"I found the contrast between the poverty I witnessed there, and the over-consumption and sense of entitlement I see here, very difficult to square with my own ethical sensibilities," he continues, gesturing at the smiling faces on the large bright canvases surrounding you. "I decided to do something to help, as far as I am able. I have used my money to build, and staff and equip, a hospital and three schools."

As he speaks, you see the same look of intensity on his face you saw in the articles which showed him painting. He is frowning slightly, as he runs his fingers through his steel grey hair, and his gaze moves over the pictures behind you. "I think it's extraordinary that we spend billions trying to establish if there is water on Mars, when there are tens of millions of humans who don't have access to clean water on earth."

"So, you see, these paintings are more than art. They represent a pictorial record of my friends, of my life's work, of possibly the one truly useful thing I have done on this earth. This isn't the kind of thing I display. I keep my work and my life separate."

You congratulate him on capturing the emotional response of the sitters. He smiles at you, sips his tea, and stares directly at you for some time without speaking.

You return his gaze. He smiles again, "Emotion is what a good artist capture. Look at Picasso - he pulls emotion from a few lines. That takes real skill. My work is of a lower order by far, I don't want you to think I'm making the comparison. But I work hard to capture feeling in my work. Would you like to see some more of my personal work? I think you will appreciate it."

You say that you would very much like to see more of his work. He rises, takes your teacup from you, and gestures for you to follow him. You walk some 20 yards further into the vast building. He stops in front of ten or so canvases laid against the wall, sufficiently large that the top third of each canvas is covering the bottom of a window.

Each painting is covered with a sheet. As you stand before them, he pulls back the first sheet. What you see makes you gasp involuntarily.

The painting depicts a woman, tied face down on a table. Other than stockings and a garter belt, she is completely naked. The artist had structured the painting in such a way that the viewers eyes were drawn to her face, which is contorted in ecstasy. Her back was arched, partially because the other subject in the painting, a man, was pulling her long blonde hair. He was also fucking her - you can see every vein in his thick, hard cock, as he is evidently about to thrust it deep inside her.

The man's face is indistinct - it seems half in shadow, but his muscular legs and torso are certainly similar to the artist that stands before you. The style is hyper-realistic -it could almost be a photograph. You find the picture powerfully affecting, and an incredible turn-on. You feel your nipples hardening at the sight, particularly because you suspect that the man in the picture is the same one that stands before you, enjoying your reaction.

"What do you think?" He asks, smiling. "Not quite the style of my public work, is it? And yet, I think you will agree that I have captured the emotion of the moment perfectly."

You nod, and say that you like it a great deal, your voice thick with what you acknowledge to yourself is desire. Desire to be in exactly the position depicted.

"Would you like to see more?", he asks, and you nod your reply, acutely aware of his intense blue eyes on yours.

He pulls the covers off several more paintings. In one, the man is lying back on the floor, and a woman, dressed in a black skirt and silk blouse, just like yours, is riding him - her skirt up around her waist, her blouse open. The man's fingers are on her nipples, obviously pinching them, and the look on her face is of intense pleasure. One of her hands is on the man's chest, the other is pulling her panties to one side and guiding his cock inside her. Again, the man's face is in shadow, turned away from the viewers gaze.

The third picture has a woman, completely naked, her hands between her legs, which are spread wide open, the same man, judging by his body, is straddling her chest, holding her glistening breasts in his hands as he fucks them. The moment has been frozen at the point that his cock is at her mouth, her head bent to flick her tongue over his glans.

Another canvas is uncovered. This one is a close-up view of a woman's ass and lower back - the man's cock is halfway inside her, and there is an unmistakable red handprint on her left cheek. Neither face can be seen in this one, but the realism of the picture, and it's subject, bring a slight moan unbidden to your lips.

"You will have seen many of my portraits, I am sure," he says, "the relationship between an artist and his sitter can be intense. Sometimes, if my subject wishes it, it passes into a physical relationship, and these pictures are the result of that. The faces you see here are the same faces that adorn offices and homes of rich men, who have no idea that I have captured their wives from a very different viewpoint."

You ask him why the man's face is in shadow, and if he is the man depicted. "That's an excellent question. It is me; these pictures are uniquely personal. In fact, you're the first woman who has seen more than one of them. I'm still not sure why I showed them to you. I think perhaps because your reaction to my Malawian pictures showed a true understanding of what it is to capture a moment of existential truth, of authenticity. I like that. That, and the undeniable fact that I find you extraordinarily attractive. I would love to paint you......"

You smile, and tell him he hasn't answered your question about why his face is in shadow. "Yes, that deserves an answer," he smiles, gazing up at one of the pictures, "I give each of my sitters a photograph of their painting. They know it's me. But they can also imagine that it is anybody they choose. That generates many more erotic possibilities for them, and I prefer that - what is hidden is often more exciting than what is displayed, no?"

You smile and nod. You ask him if the ties in the first picture were his idea, or hers. "Ah. Another excellent question. You do like to get to the heart of the matter, don't you? I flirt with BDSM, of course - not in any depth - I have never found a partner in whom I perceive the total trust required between lovers that is needed. But many women have read the execrable 50 shades books, and seek at least a taste of that experience. I am happy to provide it."

"The experiences that people remember most sharply are those where we are taken to the edge of the void, where all control is apparently lost. Let us take the example of parachuting, or bungee jumping. In an amateur, these things generate sheer terror, and although there is exhilaration, it is that of the fairground ride, a temporary increase in adrenaline that fools the uninitiated into thinking they have conquered death."

"A few hardier and more reflective individuals recognize the experience for what it is. A sensation to be embraced and refined, and finally mastered - and those are the ones who wring the greatest sensation from these activities. The same applies to sex - most people are satisfied with simply achieving orgasm. But I am prepared to push the boundaries, to approach the edge of the void, to achieve a greater satisfaction. I sense that you might be prepared to push those boundaries too."

You reply that you have never tried it, and he smiles and shakes his head. "That's not a worthy answer, and you know it - the majority of the ladies in the pictures I showed you had never been in those positions either. You pressed me for answers, now I feel entitled to a response...."

You reply that you have often thought about it, but never taken it further than that. "Ah, well, since the thought is father to the action you are most of the way there. Let me paint you. I promise nothing more unless you desire it."

At that moment you desire nothing more than to be taken right there, bent over his sofa. But you tell him you will consider it, and he leads you back to the elevator, kissing your hand - an extraordinarily old-fashioned gesture, but which feels somehow appropriate from this Scot.

A day later you receive a package at your home office. On opening it you find a note. It reads 'Please come and sit for me. You are too beautiful not to be captured for posterity. If you want nothing more than to be painted it shall be as you wish. But if you think you might like to go further, please wear the enclosed for your sitting.'

You peel back the layers of delicate tissue paper. Within is a pair of black lace and silk panties. The kind of expensive work that contrives to make a thin slip of material worth 300 pounds. And a black brassiere, again in black silk and lace. Both are exquisite, and you check the size to realise he has got them exactly right.

This is obviously a man who knows how to read a woman's body......

Beneath the lingerie is a card with a time and date on it. The date is the next day, and the time is 7pm. You drop the card and note back in the box, and place it in your desk drawer. You attempt to get on with some work, but now all you can think about is sitting for this man. This man you hardly know, but who attracts and excites you in a way you didn't think possible on so short an acquaintance.

The next day you wake early and sit at your breakfast table with some coffee. You know you have a decision to make, but you also know that you have already made it. You decided as soon as he revealed that first painting. You will sit for him. Wear what he has sent you. See what the evening brings beyond that.

That evening you take a long shower, and dress carefully- pulling on the lingerie he sent you, it feels feather-light and beautifully soft against your skin. You choose a black dress, tight in all the right places. You have no jewellery on, and no makeup. If he wants to paint you, you know he won't want you pre-painted......

You climb into your car, driving in your usual fast but controlled style. You arrive 5 minutes early, but you don't get out. You can feel your heartbeat - the rate is elevated, and you have a final argument with yourself, but you know you came this far for a reason, and the outcome of your internal dialogue is assured.

You ring the bell, and the door clicks open. He comes down in the lift to meet you once more. He is dressed in a white tee-shirt, tight against his chest, and black trousers. There is no paint on his clothes tonight.

He escorts you into the elevator, taking you by the hand. The feel of his hand on yours sets your heart beating quickly again. You can feel the tension between you, but try to be as casual as possible.

"I'm so glad you came," he says, "I wasn't completely sure that you would." You reply that you weren't sure you would either, but that you had never been painted, and you thought any new experience was worth trying. He smiles, and looks you directly in the eye, a twinkle in his intense blue eyes....

"That's what I hoped," he says, and opens the elevator door. The scene is very different from your daytime visit. Instead of blazing sunshine, the room is lit from above by the moon and stars, aside from an alcove a third of the way down, which has bright while lighting from a couple of studio lamps on stands.

He leads you to a chaise in black velvet which is set against the wall between the two lights. "Please make yourself comfortable," he says "I shall want you to hold your pose while I make my preliminary sketches, and I don't want you to suffer any discomfort."

He offers you champagne from an ice bucket that sits by the chaise. You accept a glass, and settle back on the chaise, laying on your left side, and acutely aware now of your bare arms, and that your dress reaches only to your knees....

He picks up a large sketching pad and pencil, and gazes intently at you. You had been looked at by men before, of course. Some furtive glances, some frank appraisal, some leering, but never with the intensity that this man is looking at you. His eyes take in every part of you, and his attention makes you feel extraordinarily connected to him. Never before has a man focused so deeply on your face, your eyes, your body.

He begins to sketch, and as he does so, he says "in the interests of full disclosure, and since I abhor any idea that I might make you do something you didn't truly want to do, I gave you the champagne to relax you. I know it's difficult to model for an artist - not everyone can bear the level of attention. But I don't want you to think I'm trying to get you drunk. In fact, if you did, I would put you in a cab and send you home. But I do want you to be relaxed enough to be yourself."

You thank him for his words, and tell him that one glass won't impair your faculties. He smiles at the expression, and asks you about your earliest memory. You tell him, and as he sketches, and you converse about life and art and fast cars, and you relax completely.

You know that he wants you. You know that you want him. Every atom in your body cries out for the touch of his lips on yours, his strong hands on your skin. Watching him sketch, his eyes moving between your face and the pad, you begin to fantasise about being taken the way you saw in the first picture he showed you.

You lift your right leg to get comfortable, your dress slides down your thigh, revealing bare flesh, and the lingerie he sent you. You make no move to pull it back up. In fact, you open your legs wider, so he can see.

"I see you chose to wear what I sent you," he says "I am very glad. A woman as beautiful as you should wear the most beautiful clothes. That's something Parisian women seem to do instinctively, whereas most women seem to be able to make a Chanel dress look like a sack. You, I am glad to say, are able to carry anything off. If I dressed you in a sack, you would make it look like a Chanel dress."

You smile and sip your champagne. He comes to sit at the end of the chaise, and brushes the back of his hand from the ankle of your right leg to halfway up your thigh, slowly and gently.......

The feeling is indescribably sensual. Your leg falls open further, inviting him to move higher. He smiles and says "Not yet, all in due time. First, I think we can discard the dress, don't you think?"

You nod, not quite able to trust yourself to speak, lest it comes out as a less than sexy croak. Your throat feels tight, your heart is pounding. You rise from the chaise, and allow him to unzip your dress, letting it fall to the floor. The room is warm, despite the cool evening - the studio lamps giving out substantial heat as well as light.

His eyes linger over your body, clothed only now in the lingerie he had chosen for you. "Turn around for me," he says, and you do so, knowing his eyes are on you, you bend over and place your hands on the chaise. He makes an appreciative sound - he may even have said "oh my God" under his breath, you can't quite catch it......

"You are quite as exquisite as I had imagined," he says, as you lay back on the chaise. "Your bone structure is beautiful, and your body is perfect. Any of the great masters would have considered themselves fortunate to have had you sit for them."

He sketches some more, his eyes running over your body. The champagne, the warm lights, his attention, and your own anticipation is turning you on. You run your tongue over your lips, biting your lower lip. You want to distract him from his sketching, so you slide your left leg off the chaise, spreading your right leg.

Now you are wide open to him, and a gathering dampness is evident on the almost transparent filmy silk.

"Not yet," he smiles down at you "there is another step yet for you to take." You look up at him, wondering what is next. He dips down to draw a small bag from under the chaise. He takes two metal handcuffs from the bag. They look like an ordinary pair of cuffs, such as a policeman might carry, but are not connected. They are not silver, but black, and there is a black ribbon tied to each cuff......

Your eyes widen, and you open your mouth to tell him you won't wear them. But he places a finger on your lips. It is all you can do to stop yourself from taking it in your mouth.

"I'm going to show you," he says, threading the silk from one cuff through a tiny loop at the side of your panties, and tying a knot, so that the cuff is now attached to the right side.

"Take a look at this loop of silk," he says, pointing to where the cuff is attached. "Can you see that it is only attached by two threads?" You see that there are only two thin cotton threads holding the loop, and therefore the cuffs, to your panties. You nod.

He smiles, "you understand what that means, don't you? It means that you will wear the cuffs, and be restrained, only because you want to be. At any time, you can free your hands. But if you choose to be cuffed, I think you will keep them on. I think you want to."

He attaches the other cuff to your left side, tying the silk tight within its loop. He snaps the cuffs open "the moment of truth," he says, his eyes on yours. You nod, afraid to give your desire away by speaking, and offer your right wrist to be cuffed. He clicks the cuff into place, and then cuffs your left wrist.

The feeling once you are cuffed is powerful. You feel simultaneously imprisoned and completely free. Whatever he does to you now, whatever you allow to be done to you, you can rationalize that you were helpless. And yet, you have never felt more empowered sexually.

He returns to his pad, and continues his sketching. You pout at him, wanting his hands on you, not his eyes.

He smiles. "I'm almost done," he says, as you let your legs fall open, inviting him to stare between your legs, to see how wet you already are.

He puts his pad down. Steps out of his shoes, strips off his tee shirt and trousers. He is wearing neither sock not shorts. Your eyes take in the details of his body as he strips. It is as depicted in the pictures you have seen. He has powerful looking legs, the calves as thick as your thighs. His chest is large, his shoulders and upper arms are well muscled, but not bulky. He carries no middle-aged spread.

His cock is already hard. It looks thick and long, the head swollen, and you imagine what it will feel like inside you, in your hands, your mouth....

He kneels by the side of the chaise, and brings his lips to yours, just brushing your lips gently, his hand on your cheek. You lift your head for a deeper kiss, wanting to increase his desire for you, and you kiss deeply and passionately. He bites your lower lip gently, and his hand trails gently down your neck, cupping your right breast.

He unfastens your brassiere- it has a front opening, and you watch his face as your breasts are revealed to him, the nipples hard and aching for his touch. He lifts his eyes to yours, "you are magnificent," he says, and bends his head to take your nipple in his mouth.

As his lip's envelope your nipple, you feel the shock of the cold ice he has taken from the ice bucket. As he sucks your nipple, gently biting it, the alternate hot and ice-cold sensations send a palpable sensation directly between your legs. You want this man to take you. To make you come, perhaps more than you ever have before....

He takes your other nipple in his mouth, massaging the first between finger and thumb as he sucks and bites, your breath now shallow, desperate to feel him inside you.

He comes back to your mouth for a kiss, both of you now hungry for each other. He reaches under the chaise again, and comes out with a brush, in a pot of water. It is around the size of a pencil in length and thickness, although the bristles are approximately the width of his thumb, as he holds it up to show you.

"I told you I wanted to paint you, and I do," he says, "this is a Kolinsky Sable brush. They are soft yet strong, and for fine work they are impossible to replicate artificially- and you, I think, are the finest work I shall ever do."

He dips the brush in the water, then brushes your nipples with it. The softness of the bristles, coupled with their flexibility, and the cool of the water under the warm lights, makes you gasp with lust at the sensation produced....

He moves down between your legs.... Brushing your thighs lightly, the feeling making you open your legs wider to his touch. You are already wet, the silk of your panties soaked, he pulls them down at the front, revealing your clit with his fingers spread on both side of it.

Then you gasp as he brushes your clit. The brush wet with your juices; the feeling is incredible. You can feel your orgasm building, as he swirls the brush around your clit, then from top to bottom, the softness of the bristles driving your desire to new heights, his fingers bringing pressure from the sides.

He is watching you closely, and just as you are about to come, your muscles taught, your head thrown back, he removes the brush. You moan with disappointment, and it is all you can do to prevent yourself from tearing your hands free and reaching for your clit to achieve your climax.

"Not yet," he smiles, "I know you wanted to break free there, and yet you held back, and that's because you know the longer you leave it, the more I tease you, take you close to the edge, when your release does come, it will be so much stronger."

He moves down between your legs now, lifting your hips with his strong hands as he buries his face between your legs, your back arched, feeling the heat from his tongue through the silk, hot against your soaking lips. You moan again, feeling your orgasm close as he pulls your panties down at the front and slides his tongue over your clit, but again he pulls back at the last moment, leaving you frustrated.

Now he kneels before you, his cock sliding over your panties. You can feel how hot and hard he is through the wet silk. "These have a secret design feature," he tells you, sliding his fingers over the strip of silk overlaying your wetness, "which I myself specified with the designer."

He finds the hole which is concealed at the front of your panties, a hole which is a concealed entry, a thin tunnel of silk which he inserts his hard cock through, the damp silk dragging against his cock. The tunnel of silk ends inside your panties - bringing his cock directly in contact with your soaking lips.

He pulls the top of them down, so you can both watch his cock sliding over your lips, and the swollen head nudging your clit. Then he replaces the material, and begins to rock his hips back and forth, controlling the movement of your body with his hands. This enables him to target your clit with his cock, rolling the hot head across your clit, sliding the roughness of the shaft over it, the silk material pressing his cock hard into your clit.

He fucks your clit, reaching across to pick up the paintbrush, which he drags across your nipples as he fucks you. The sensation is unlike any other you have ever experienced, and you watch as his cock slides over you, feeling every millimeter of movement at your very core.

All sensation, all thought, is now concentrated between your legs. You have to come; you need it now more than you need air. You look into his eyes, with mute appeal, unwilling to break the spell. "What do you want?" he asks you, smiling.

"I want you to fuck me," you reply, desperate to feel him inside you. "Say please," he replies "please, oh God, please," you gasp, as he pulls his cock away from your clit. "Beg me," he says, that intense look in his blue eyes returning "beg me to fuck you."

"Fuck me," you gasp "I'm begging you to fuck me. Fucking take me you bastard."

With that, he slides his hot, hard cock inside you. You wrap your legs around him, pulling him into you, and as he leans down to take your nipples in his mouth, you come so hard you can barely breathe.

He pulls out of you, turns you over, so you are kneeling face down on the chaise. He rips your panties, so that they are now just a strip of material around your waist, and slides his hard cock just an inch inside you. He reaches down for the paint brush again, and as he slowly slides his cock inside you, he drags the wet bristles over your clit, the feeling incredible as you feel the sensation of his cock inside you, and the firm but light strokes of the brush.

Your arms are still pinned to your sides, and you are on your face, your ass in the air as he fucks you. You come hard again as he reaches around to rub your clit, moaning like an animal with the strength of your climax. He grabs you by the upper arms, lifting your body as he fucks you harder and deeper now, each stroke ending with him slamming the base of his cock against you. You can feel another orgasm building, and you come again, gasping with pure lust as wave after wave of your climax overtakes you.

He pulls out of you again, pulls you to your feet, lays you on your back on the chaise, and places each of your ankles on his shoulders. He slides his cock over you, now completely soaking, and open to him.

He looks down at you as he slides his cock halfway inside you, and as he sees you plead with your eyes, he slams his cock hard and deep into you. He reaches for the brush again, and for some ice from the champagne bucket.

He alternates the ice on your clit, with the brush, the warmth from your own juices and the friction counteracting the cold of the ice, heightening the feeling as his cock slams into you, hard and fast, urgent now, his control lost as he fucks you, pounding himself into you. You watch him closely, his head thrown back, his teeth bared like a wolf. It is then that you break your bonds, pulling his ass into you, digging your nails in as you thrust your hips up to meet his, feeling the spasm as he pours himself into you, thrust after thrust as he comes deep inside you, and as your rub your clit, you come again, your fingers in his mouth......

You lay together for some time, talking of Barcelona, places you have been, and he invites you to meet him in Barcelona in a month. You tell him you will think about it.

But your decision is already made......

Wheel Of Motion

Julie sat quietly and calmly in a private booth watching the door of Lacey's Club. Half concealed in the shadows thrown by the dim light Julie reflected on the exchange of e-mails over the past months. When she had mentioned the forthcoming trip to New York the other two women had insisted she visited Lacey's. Unlike many places these days the private status meant the members could smoke, and although not a member Julie had been invited in as her name had been left on the guest list at the door. She was surprised at the difference shown to her by the hostess when she gave her name, and the knowing smile as she showed her to the booth in the back of the room.

The smoke from Julie's Marlboro curled up into the lights and she calmly watched the couples at different tables. There wasn't a man in the place but Julie had known it was a lesbian club before she came and was very comfortable with it. She felt a little nervous perhaps but also excited and had dressed especially for the occasion. The short black leather dress was tight in all the right places and split wickedly up the front so that it was nearly at her crotch when she sat down.

The door opened and Julie knew straight away it was the two she was waiting for. Cassie was the shorter of the two and her blonde hair framed her pretty face. She was wearing black cowgirl boots, tight black leather pants and a shearling coat. Vanessa was taller at almost six feet, with dark brunette hair. She was wearing black thigh-high platform boots and blue jeans. To guard against the cold, she was wearing a full-length leather trench coat. She reached into her coat pocket and took out a pack of More cigarettes and a lighter. She placed the sexy long brown cigarette between her lips and casually lit it. Her slim gloved fingers now wrapped around the cigarette as she pulled the smoke deep into her lungs. The warm smoke was soothing, and she exhaled slowly through her mouth and nose.

Julie was hot with anticipation as she saw the two women moving towards her, but suddenly, her view was blocked by a figure looming in front of her. At first, she thought it was a man. Then she realized it was a bull dyke, dressed in a man's suit and fedora. "I'm Wanda," she said. "How about we go to the bathroom and I show you a good time."

Julie was a little concerned by her situation as she would like to deal with matters quietly, but then she saw her two friends approach, and Vanessa tapped Wanda on her shoulder. As Wanda whirled around Vanessa snarled, " Wait your turn, bitch,"

With that Vanessa took a deep drag on her cigarette, and blew a mouthful of creamy smoke into Wanda's face. Julie wasn't really afraid, but surprised at how aroused she was getting to see the women fight over her. Wanda opened up her jacket to reveal a large knife. "Get lost, or I'll slice your nipples off," she threatened.

Julie saw the knife and moved her hand instinctively to the small of her back and then cursed when she remembered that she was abroad and therefore not armed. Julie measured the distance between herself and Wanda and with a sinking feeling realised that starting from a sitting position was not ideal. Coiling her body like a spring Julie prepared herself mentally for the violent explosion when she saw Vanessa and Cassie smile at each other and opened their own coats. Both Julie and Wanda could see the gun in Vanessa's shoulder holster and the one in Cassie's hip holster.

Wanda's mouth opened in terror as she started to back away.

Vanessa smiled at Wanda. "Smart move cunt," she snarled. "It would be a shame to see what brains you have splattered all over the wall."

Where Julie lived, even the police did not routinely carry guns and to her surprise, her nipples were hard in anticipation as she watched her new friends ready to kill to protect her. She felt safe and warm with these two caring for her.

As Wanda skulked away to try her luck with another femme, Vanessa turned to Julie. "So you are Julie then" Vanessa purred as she held out her hand, "Cassie has told me a lot about you, and was wondering how much was true."

Julie just smiled and moving slightly opened her long legs clad in black boots causing the split in the dress to open more. Vanessa's face split into a wide smile as she saw Julie was naked under her dress.

"Hiya hun" Cassie said as she joined the table then smiled as well as she saw the view that Vanessa was getting.

The two women slid in either side of Julie and ordered champagne from the waitress who had appeared. While they waited for the waitress to return, they engaged on small talk: how were you, flight, your hotel OK, etc. As they talked, Cassie and Vanessa looked at each other knowingly. They had anticipated this problem and would have to deal with it.

Over the years, they had become addicted to BBC programs that were shown on cable TV. These ranged form adaptation of classic novels, to mysteries and comedies. But they all had one thing in common: they were unintelligible and the girls had to watch with closed-captioning subtitles. As Julie continued to describe her trip, they both thought the same thing: "Why the fuck can't these people speak proper English?"

The waitress finally arrived with the Dom Perignon, uncorked the bottle, and poured for each of them. Julie saw the wistful look in the waitress's eyes, wishing she could join them, but knowing she couldn't.

"So you sure you want this to happen?" Vanessa asked staring into Julie's blue eyes, resting her arm on Julie's shoulder.

"Sure she does" Cassie smiled, "otherwise she wouldn't be sitting there all dressed up like a Christmas present in leather."

As the two women began to share their day with each other, Julie relaxed and then felt a hand on either knee climbing slowly upwards. Julie simply opened her legs and allowed the exploration to continue and wondered what would happen when their fingers met which was pretty close to happening.

As their fingers touched Cassie stopped talking and smiled broadly at Vanessa who smiled back. Then in unison both women pushed a finger each into Julie's body and she couldn't suppress a moan of pleasure as they worked their way in. Julie's body stiffened as two of Vanessa's fingers penetrated her and found the little ridge that was so packed with very sensitive nerve endings, the G-spot. Meanwhile, Cassie's index finger adventured farther north, found Julie's hood, and then probed under it to find her hidden clit. Julie's back arched again as Cassie's finger found its target. Julie writhed under their touch as Vanessa stretched her pussy and massaged the ridge with the tips of her fingers, and Cassie twisted and tweaked at her clit.

"What are you doing?" Julie moaned as a flood of lubricating fluid met Vanessa's fingers.

"We're just checking your size and seeing if you're ready," Cassie teased. They pulled their fingers out from their guest's pussy. Looking seductively at Julie, they licked their wet fingers, and then dipped their cum-laden fingers in their champagne. As Cassie and Vanessa raised their glasses to toast her, Julie noticed her juices mixing with the bubbly liquid in their glasses.

Cassie leant forward and whispered in Julie's left ear, "Our apartment is just round the corner."

Vanessa whispered in the other ear, "The only question is who gets your ass and who gets your pussy."

Giggling softly Julie purred, "You will just have to take turns won't you."

It was a short walk back to their apartment block and soon the three of them were inside the well-appointed apartment. The view over New York's skyline was breathtaking and the two women smiled at Julie as Cassie said, "Make yourself at home, we just need to slip into something more comfortable," and with that they disappeared into the bedroom. Julie looked out the other window with its spectacular view of Central Park, covered in a fresh blanket of snow.

Julie looked round and could tell from the quality that the two of them were clearly very successful. She was examining the books in the book case when she heard Vanessa say, "That's better, much more comfortable."

Turning Julie saw that both of them had stripped off and were both wearing shiny black leather thigh-high boots with 6-inch spiked heels. Julie let out a gasp as she saw the sight of her new friends in their come-fuck-me boots. From the look of their closely cropped landing strips, Julie could see that Vanessa was a natural brunette, and Cassie a natural blond.

Vanessa giggled as she saw that Julie's mouth was wide open. "On the floor, baby" she ordered Julie, " and get what's coming to you!"

Julie lay down on the rug and spread her legs in anticipation as Cassie lit a cigarette and knelt down between her knees. She took a puff on her cigarette and then placed her mouth over Julie's pussy. Julie's body twitched as the warm smoke rolled over her pussy, and then gasped as Cassie's tongue started exploring her inner thigh. Vanessa leaned over Julie, and their lips locked. Vanessa opened her mouth and extended her tongue into Julie's inviting mouth. Their tongues met and Julie tried to match Vanessa thrust for thrust. Slowly and seductively, Cassie was moving up higher and higher, pushing up Julie's dress to gain better access. Her tongue now found Julie's labia, swollen in anticipation. With her two hands, Cassie spread Julie's lips, and waited for Vanessa. Vanessa took a swig of ice-cold vodka, and bent over and placed her mouth over Julie's right nipple. Julie screamed as Vanessa's ice-cold mouth encased her nipple and her tongue flicked at her nipple, which was already rock-hard. The scream was Cassie's signal, and as she plunged her tongue into Julie's pussy, Julie's body quivered involuntarily as the two girls worked on her, stimulating her erogenous zones with their fingers and tongues.

They held her down tightly as she squirmed with each thrust, with each lick, with each kiss. As Vanessa continued to kiss Julie and fondle her breast, Cassie blew another mouthful of smoke into her pussy and started to manipulate her hood.

"I can't take it, anymore! I'm going to explode!" Julie cried. "Fuck me now and fuck me hard," she pleaded.

Cassie lifted her head up. "I thought you'd never ask, darling," she giggled. "We'll be back in one minute."

Julie got to her knees, and was a little dizzy from the cigarette smoke and the alcohol, but mostly, it was from these two women who had taken charge of her like no one else ever had. Oh, she had been with women before, and she was usually the dominant one. Despite her experience, she had never been this out-of-control, never pleaded ---she had actually begged-- for someone to fuck her.

As she got to her knees, Vanessa and Cassie had come back with their gear. With a sly smile, Vanessa handed Julie another glass of champagne, then turned with her back to Cassie. She stepped into a strap-on harness, and then played with her own nipples as Cassie positioned it, tightened the straps and made sure it was snug and secure. Then they changed places, and Cassie now had hers in place.

They stood there, confronting Julie and helped her to her feet. "You ready for the big ride?" Cassie teased.

Julie nodded silently as she recalled how she had described to Cassie in graphic detail in various e-mails how she would like to be fucked by two women. Julie moved to strip and Cassie laughed as she said, "Oh no hun stay just as you are, thought it would be nice if that dress unlaced at the front."

Julie undid the laced front allowing her breasts to spill free. Her nipples were still rock hard, and they giggled as they saw the hickey Vanessa had given her right breast.

"I'll just be one minute darling," Cassie said as she lay on her back, her knees bent to expose her crotch and Julie saw that Vanessa was now lubricating a strap-on. On a closer look, she saw it was no ordinary one. The outer strap-on was 8 inches long and quite thick, and then she saw the inner dong and the remote. Vanessa handed the toy to Cassie who closed her eyes, and with a practiced feel, slipped the inner dong into her pussy. Cassie grunted as the dong found it's place inside her and she locked the strap-on into position on the harness.

Vanessa moved behind Julie and holding her shoulders tightly, pushed her down on her knees in front of Cassie. "On your knees, bitch!" she commanded. "And take her deep!"

For Julie, this was a dream come true, and she gabbed the shaft of Cassie's cock and started to lick it at a furious pace. Then, as Vanessa started fondling her from behind, she took Cassie's cock deep in her throat. After just a few minutes, it was more than Julie could take and with pleading eyes, she looked at Cassie. "I need you inside me! Please."

Cassie laughed, and held the strapon upwards by the base. "Hop on hun" she purred.

Julie had to pull the dress up over her hips to get her legs wide enough and straddled Cassie's body. Vanessa placed her arms around Julie to steady her and to get another feel of her tits. Julie's pussy was still soaked from the foreplay that had started in the bar and easing down teased her pussy lips on the head. Cassie reached up and holding Julie's hips pulled her down until she was fully impaled. A long sigh of pleasure escaped Julie's lips as she felt the strapon deep inside her and Cassie also moaned as Julie's pressure on the strap-on pushed the inner dong deep into her pussy and against her G-spot.

For Cassie and Vanessa, this was one of their favourite sex toys; the better you fucked your partner, the better you fucked yourself. Cassie started to make gentle upwards movements of her hips as Julie pushed down to meet her thrusts. As she became wetter, Julie started to ride the strapon harder lifting up until it almost left her body then pushing down hard. And with each movement of the strapon, there was a corresponding thrust of the inner dong inside Cassie.

Cassie and Julie were now synchronizing their thrusts Cassie heard a familiar moan and knew that Vanessa's dong and strapon were in place. Julie felt the orgasm begin to rise in her body and almost screamed in frustration when she felt a hand on her back stopping her movements. That was Cassie's cue and she put her arms around Julie's neck and pulled her towards her, and raised up her legs and wrapped her boots around Julie's midsection. Cassie was always amazed that these strapons were so firm and so flexible. When she had been with guys, any rapid change in position would make them lose it. Even at this angle, her strapon was still fitting snugly in Julie's pussy.

Holding Julie firmly in place, Cassie now locked lips with her. As their tongues heatedly explored each other's mouths, Cassie felt Julie's body shudder as Vanessa applied the cold gel to her ass,

"It's time baby," Vanessa murmured as she probed first one then two fingers into Julie's ass. Julie squirmed on Cassie's strapon as she felt the probing become deeper and more intense. Vanessa was making sure that Julie was being well stretched and lubricated before she plunged her cock deep into her. As Julie squirmed under Vanessa's touch, the strapon moved in and out of her pussy and the dong in and out of Cassie's.

When Vanessa finished the lube job and pulled her fingers out, Julie's body tensed as she realized what was coming next. The head of the strapon felt tight against her ass and Julie breathed deeply to relax and as she did so the head slipped in.

"Ahhhhhh fuckkkkkkkk" Julie exclaimed.

"Feels good don't it." Vanessa said softly as she pushed the strapon deeper and deeper into Julie's ass until it was fully home. This set off a chain of reactions. As the strapon penetrated deep in Julie's ass, Vanessa's inner dong was forced deep into her pussy. And as the forward pressure pushed Julie into taking Cassie's strap-on deeper into her pussy, Cassie's doing was forced into her, too.

Julie was now trapped between the two women, with Cassie having wrapped her booted legs against Julie's middle and Vanessa straddling her ass and fucking it with her strapon. Satisfied that they were all positioned properly, Vanessa said, "OK let's ride."

That was the signal for both of them to activate the battery pack switches. As the strapons began to vibrate in her pussy and asshole, Julie began to rock back and forth, as Cassie and Vanessa started to feel the buzzing in their own pussies, they joined Julie in a rhythmic back and forth motion, with each thrust setting off the chain reaction stimulation. With that Vanessa pulled back and Julie felt herself lift partially upwards before

Vanessa firmly drove the strapon back into her ass forcing her down onto Cassie's strapon.

"Oh my fucking god," Julie exclaimed as she felt herself being filled in both holes. Vanessa and Cassie began to fuck Julie in earnest and with each pull back Cassie pushed upwards and then inwards as Vanessa forced Julie back down. The movements became harder and more forceful as Julie relaxed more and more until at one point both strapons nearly left her body and then both plunged deep at the same time.

That pushed Julie over the top and screaming loudly bucked and writhed as the two women kept up their steady fucking. Orgasm after orgasm burst in Julie's brain until she felt she would pass out from the pleasure. Now, Cassie and Vanessa started to feel their orgasms starting and Julie was confused as she had just had one of the best set of orgasms in her life and she was still being fucked and she felt that she was going to start up all over again.

Cassie could feel her nipples becoming very hard and her pussy was now wet. Vanessa continued to lean forward applying constant pressure to Julie's rectum and Cassie moved her hips upward to propel her cock into Julie's pussy. Cassie began to moan as the dong rocked back and forth inside her pussy, and she now felt herself beginning to cum. Her pussy began to pulsate in increasingly powerful contractions. They seemed to be more potent, intense, and longer than any she had experienced before. The intensity was incredibly overwhelming! "OOOOH MY GOD!" she screamed. "YES! YES! OOOOOHH YEEEEEEESSSS!" She writhed around in uncontrolled ecstasy, her pussy contracting and contracting in wave after mind-blowing wave of extreme pleasure. "OOOOOOOOH FUCK! OOOOH GOOOOOORD, YEEEES! YES, YEEEEEES!" Cassie continued to scream in ecstasy

Meanwhile, Vanessa was starting to cum and was bucking her hips up and down, pounding Julie's rectum with abandon. As the first wave hit her, Vanessa's face was contorted in rapture as it consumed her totally. Each successively powerful contraction left her gasping and screaming in unrestrained exaltation, "ahh..ahhh..AHHHH..Yesss Yessssss.."

As Vanessa's body contorted in ecstasy, she heard Cassie scream, " I'm coming again!"

"Me, too," Julie moaned

"That makes three," Vanessa thought to herself as he own orgasm burst again.

As Vanessa and Cassie continued to thrust their cocks into Julie, and the dongs into themselves, their pussy muscles started contracting simultaneously. All three of them were writhing and screaming and cumming in unison.

"OOOOOOOOOOOOOH YEEEEEES, YEEEEEES!" Cassie screamed.

"ahhh..ohhhh..AHHHHH Yeahhh oh Yeahhhh!" Julie moaned.

"Fuck me like a whore!" Vanessa squealed as she started to cum again.

Their pussies continued to explode. Spasm after spasm violently engulfed them as they fucked back and forth in rampant, unrestrained rapture.

"YEEEES! OOOOOOOOOOH! YEEEEEEEEEEEEEEEEEEES!!!!!!!!" Julie shrieked as she collapsed on top of Cassie in exhaustion.

Eventually, the waves of pleasure began to subside. Vanessa slipped her strapon cock out of Julie's ass and pulled her off Cassie's strapon. . Cassie looked up at the two of them. "Oh, fucking Jesus Christ!" she moaned as she tried to stand, but was still a little shaky and collapsed back to lie next to Cassie and Vanessa. "That was fucking unbelievable! It was fucking out of this world!"

The three women lay silently next to each other trying to regain their breath. Vanessa kissed Julie gently on the back of her neck as Cassie kissed Julie's face. Then Cassie whispered softly, "See two into one does go."

Julie looked at the two of them and whimpered pleadingly, "I'm ready to go again."

Vanessa looked at Cassie and smiled. They had found a new and wonderful fuck buddy.

Witty Sunday

I hate football. I mean I really despise football. Which is almost a heresy in the south, but it is true. The only thing worse than the NFL football season is the NFL playoffs...and the only thing worse than the NFL playoffs, is the playoffs when your husband's team is in them.

My husband, a Wisconsin transplant, is a die-hard Green Bay Packers fan and come Super Bowl Sunday they were in it. He is a football freak and is annoying during a normal Super Bowl, never mind a Green Bay Packers' Super Bowl Sunday. The whole two weeks before the game was spent watching hours and hours of pre-week crap.

During those two weeks, I was ignored. All I wanted was my Pink Bay Packed, if you catch my drift, which led to my own SUPER BOWL SUNDAY!

As always is the case, we hosted a few people over for the big game and also, as usual, I was to play the perfect hostess wife, a role I had been playing year after year.

For the past three years, Dianne, my best friend since she moved into our neighborhood, came over early to assist with the male drink-off. While I am a Southern Belle, born and raised, Dianne is from the north and has a much more aggressive personality than me. While I submissively wait hand and foot on my husband, she clearly is the one who wears the pants in her marriage. Regardless, by lunch we were drinking wine while preparing appetizers for the game and bitching about our husbands.

I was also just a tad anxious and nervous. It was last Super Bowl Sunday when Dianne came up behind me while I was cutting a cucumber and leaned in and wrapped her arms around me, cupping my breasts. She was drunk by then, but her forwardness stunned me. A call from my husband for another beer was enough to break the brief intimate moment as I scurried out to obey my man. Nothing had ever been said about that brief moment, although I would be lying if I said it hadn't become the trigger for many of my lesbian thoughts about my best friend. Although it seemed unlikely, since nothing had happened since that day, a small part of me was dying for it to happen again.

By two, we were on our second bottle of wine and had done our wifely duties. Our husbands and their friends were transfixed in front of the TV watching the pre-game babble. After being beckoned for more beer by my husband and obediently getting it for him, Dianne pointed out, "Your man takes you for granted."

"Not really," I defended.

"Yes, really," Dianne countered. "He treats you like a maid."

"That is just the way he grew up in his home," I rationalized.

"So," Dianne argued, "you deserve to be treated as the Goddess you are."

I blushed, not used to having flattery sent my way. I am still quite pretty for 45 and my breasts are still pretty impressive at 34C, but my husband had long quit paying attention to me.

"No seriously," Dianne continued, "stand up."

"Why?" I asked.

"Because I want to take a look at you." Standing up herself and pulling me to my feet. She gazed into my eyes and time stood still. I was like a high school girl again, waiting for that first kiss. I wanted it so bad, was sure it was coming, yet her eyes just bored into mine. I felt like she could read my soul and my desperate desire for her to touch me.

Her smile broadened and she leaned in slowly and our lips touched. Although the kiss was stunningly soft, fireworks went off in my head and wetness formed in my panties. Her tongue parted my lips and she explored my mouth with a sweet sensuality that had me weak at the knees. The kiss lasted less than a minute, but in that brief time everything changed. I wanted nothing more than to do everything with her.

She broke the kiss and whispered, "Don't move, Baby."

Even the way she called me Baby was sweet and enduring, unlike the way a man calls a woman 'Baby', like she is just some sex object.

I stood nervously as she continued fattering me in a very unorthodox way. She went behind me, squeezed my ass firmly and complimented, "Nice, firm ass". She lingered there just long enough to get me excited before continuing her appraisal. She returned to face me and continued, as she put her hands through my hair, "You still have sexy natural blonde hair." Her touch felt so nice that I felt yet another uncontrollable tingle down below. Her hands suddenly cupped my breasts, assessing, "And you have the sweetest tits around. Still firm and I bet super nice nipples." I stared at her both stunned and mesmerized by her aggressive approach.

I stood completely frozen a mixture of stunned shock and undeniable excitement overwhelming me.

"Take off your bra, Loretta" she demanded, her hand extended.

"What?" I asked, stunned by what she wanted.

"You heard me. Take off your bra for me," she repeated.

I hesitated briefly, before slowly, unhooking my bra and giving it to my best friend, my hands shaking with anxiety and curiosity.

She smiled and continued, ignoring the fact that I had just handed her my bra, "And your blue eyes, I could just stare into them forever. Loretta, you are a perfectly beautiful woman who should be treated as such."

"Thank you," I blushed, completely flattered by the special attention I was receiving.

"Now let's see those nipples," she announced, lifting up my shirt and taking a long hard look at my stiff excited nipples. "Hmmmm, long and hard as I expected," she assessed looking me in the eye and asking, ever-so-sweetly, "Do you want me to suck on them?"

Her sexy smile and her warm touch had me weak all over and I whimpered, "Yes."

She leaned forward and took my sensitive right nipple, often ignored by my husband, in her mouth. I let out a moan on contact and a chill went up my spine. Her hot breath on my nipple, mixed with the wine and the secret fantasy I had been holding in, was too much and I succumbed to the temptation and just let go. She played with my left nipple too, sucking and nibbling. My breathing began to get heavier, my breasts being my most erogenous zone, when Dianne's husband called her to bring him some snacks and she completely lost it, ending the sensual moment, "That fucking useless bastard."

She went to the fridge, found the carrots, and lifted up her skirt and quickly inserted carrot after carrot into her pussy and then onto the serving tray. Just as amazing and obscene as was the carrot thing, it came to my attention she had no panties on.

She looked up, saw me transfixed on her obscene act and ordered, "Grab a cucumber, Loretta."

I did, not even remotely considering what she had in mind.

As soon as I had it, she ordered, "Sit on the chair, baby."

Being called Baby was such a turn-on as it made me feel wanted, and I did as she requested.

"Open your legs," she instructed.

I sat frozen at her request. The carrot bag empty now, Dianne moved to me and took the cucumber from my hand. She parted my legs, pulled my panties to the side, and smiled deviously at me.

I watched in paralyzed awe as my best friend slid a long green cucumber inside my very wet pussy. Her next words were also shocking, "Hmmm, Loretta. You have a delicious looking pussy."

She leaned forward and licked my clit briefly as she slowly fucked my pussy.

When her husband called for food again, she roared, "It will be there in a couple of minutes. Now hold your fucking horses."

She smiled at me, "We are not done here yet." She pulled the shiny cucumber out of my now sopping wet pussy and cut it in half. She handed me the half that had not been in me yet and ordered, "Get that ready too, Baby."

I obediently took the cucumber and slid it back into my feverish pussy. I did a few strokes before handing it to Dianne.

She finished cutting the cucumber, added some crackers and disappeared with the pussy coated vegetables. I didn't move until she came back and smiled, "Think they will notice?"

"I doubt it," I weakly replied, my need to orgasm draining my rational thoughts. Of course, they didn't notice.

She returned to me, fell to her knees, and asked, "Do you want to come, Baby?"

"Desperately," I answered honestly.

She stared into my eyes and spoke the sweetest words I have heard in years, "You know I love you, Baby." A second later, her finger slid inside me.

"I love you too," I whimpered, knowing I was speaking the truth.

She teased, "Is that because I got you so horny?"

"No," I answered, "I have fantasized about this every since you grabbed my breasts last year."

"Really?" she asked, pumping my pussy. "If I would have known that, I would have devoured you long ago."

I moaned softly again, distracted by her finger. "Do you want me to eat your pussy, Baby?"

"Please Dianne, I need to come so badly."

She smiled and leaned forward. Her tongue did things to my body I didn't know could be done. Where my hubby was random and all over the place, Dianne explored with precision, tenderness, and care. She brushed my outer pussy lips, teasing gently. She spanked my clit with her tongue, and she parted my glistening lips and slid her tongue inside me. My moans got louder and I had to bite my lip to hold in the scream that should have followed when my orgasm hit. Her mouth sucking on my clit, I exploded my juice into my best friend's eager mouth.

She didn't let go of my clit until I begged, "Please stop, it tickles now."

She obliged, standing up and saying, "You have a delicious cunt."

I blushed at the unique flattery as I attempted to recover.

She pulled me up. She asked, "You have never been with a woman before have you?"

I shook my head no.

"But you want to please me?"

I nodded in the affirmative.

She opened her legs and whispered, "Just do what comes naturally, my love."

I desperately wanted to make her feel as good as she had made me feel. I leaned between her legs and slowly extended my tongue to her wet pussy lips. Her taste was indescribable, a sweetness that after one lick I knew I would be addicted to. I attempted to replicate what she had done to me, exploring her pussy with my tongue. As her moans increased, I moved to her clit and sucked it into my mouth.

She instantly let out a louder than anticipated, "Oh fuck, Loretta."

A chill went up my spine at the thought of making her get off and I slid a finger into her wet pussy. I quickly began pumping her pussy with my finger while still sucking on her clit.

She moaned, "Oh yes, Baby, another finger."

I obeyed, sliding a second finger easily inside her.

Within seconds of filling her pussy with my fingers, her legs stiffened and I felt a gush of her juice on my face and fingers. I eagerly continued lapping up her excess juice, savouring her taste until the very last drop.

Once her orgasm was done, she smiled, "Hmmm, I think we have started a new Super Bowl tradition."

Standing up from my sore knees, I added, "I hope this is more than just a once a year thing."

"You can bet on it," Dianne smiled, standing up and reaching for a new bottle of wine.

Another bottle of wine later and the game well under way, Dianne sipped her wine and asked, "Do you think they would shut the TV off if we walked out there naked?"

I chuckled, "Well maybe if you did. I have tried tantalizing him while a game is on, even a game not involving his beloved Packers and I get nothing. On the other hand, my hubby would be in awe of your big breasts as I know he takes peeks at your cleavage when he gets the chance."

Dianne returned the compliment. "Your hubby is a tit man and mine is a leg's man, so if you went out there in thigh high stockings and heels, he may notice."

We both laughed before Dianne had a mischievous smile cross her face.

"What?" I asked skeptically.

"Let's see if we can tempt them," she suggested.

"How so?"

"Let's go upstairs and dress up a little more provocative."

"I don't really have anything more provocative," I replied.

"Hmmmm," Dianne pondered, "I'll be right back."

She returned a few minutes later dressed completely differently. She was wearing a very low-cut shirt that left little to the imagination. I briefly stared at her double-D breasts, my mouth watering just slightly as all my year-long fantasies flashed through my head. She was now in three-inch heels and a short skirt as well.

She handed me a small bag and ordered, "Go put these on."

I stammered, "O-o-ok."

I took the bag and went upstairs. In my room I dumped the contents of the bag onto my bed and was taken aback by what Dianne expected me to wear. It was a black leather skirt, with a red blouse and black thigh high stockings. Also, because we had the same size feet, there also was a pair of fuck-me boots.

I stared at the outfit for awhile, contemplating what to do as I was way too conservative to wear such an outfit, never mind wearing such an outfit to tease a bunch of drunken men. The decision was made for me when Dianne walked into my room and asked, "Do you need some help?"

"I can't wear this."

"Not even for me?" she asked, smirking coyly.

"Well..." I weakened.

"Actually, I was thinking we should make our own half time show."

"How so?"

"Get dressed and I will tell you," she smiled.

I obeyed, getting into the sluttiest outfit I had ever worn.

"Fuck, you look hot," she complimented me once I was dressed.

"Thanks," I blushed, flattered by her every word.

"So here is the plan," she said, turning on the bedroom TV "Three minutes till half, perfect."

I looked at the score. Green Bay was up by six. "Perfect, how?"

"Well let's test our men. What is more important? Their stupid football game or their wives?

"I already know the answer to that," I sighed.

"Well, let's go downstairs and see if they notice that their wives are dressed as sluts," Dianne said.

"I already know the answer," I sighed.

Dianne grabbed my hand and led me downstairs and into the living room. There was just over a minute until half time.

Dianne walked in front of her husband who obliviously did not remotely notice his wife's scantly attire. I did the same and was, as expected, not treated as a sex object but as a hindrance. "Babe, out of the way," he ordered, waving his hands.

Dianne, her red-faced cheeks displaying her anger, said, "Loretta and I are going to make our own half time show."

Both men grunted ignoring the words, although their buddies definitely seemed to notice.

Dianne grabbed my hand and led me to her house. As soon as the door was closed, she pushed me against the door and kissed me hard. Unlike the tender kiss of earlier, this time there was a savage rawness to the passion. It made me feel wanted and desirable and I melted into her.

Breaking the kiss, she pulled me to her bedroom and pushed me onto her bed. Smiling, she went to my ear, nibbling it roughly and slowly moved down to my neck. Her concentrated sucking on my neck was amazing, but she lingered so long in one spot I worried she might leave marks. She continued her downward, meandering to my breasts, unbuttoning the red blouse she had insisted I wear. Her mouth never left my body as she slowly discarded the blouse. My breasts free, she made love to every inch of them with her lips. The excessive attention was knee-numbing and my breathing accelerated. Slowly, she moved to my tummy and swirled her tongue in my belly-button, something no one had ever done. It brought a sudden chill up my back as I waited for more.

The slow admiring of my body was driving me wild and bringing new sensations to every part of me, but mostly my mind. It was sensory overload and easily the most sexual arousal I had felt since college.

She continued her exploration of my body as she slid between my legs, her hot breath lingering on my wanton pussy. I felt her move forward, as if she planned to finally touch my needy vagina, but the sensual tease continued as she moved down and placed soft kisses on my left thigh. Her tongue and lips never left my thigh and leg as she spattered me with soft kisses.

Unzipping my boot, she gently slid it off and licked the sole of my foot. It tickled a bit, but watching her tender loving care had me gushing. She took each toe and sucked it individually through the sheer stockings, like she was pleasuring a small cock. Once she had made love to my foot, she moved to my other foot and once my boot was off, she replicated the same concentrated pleasure. Glancing at the clock, it had been half an hour since we left my house, half an hour of my body being worshipped by this beautiful woman.

By the time she began to slither her tongue back to my pussy, I was ready to grab her head and rub myself to orgasm. Thankfully, she could read my utter desperation and she moved to my pussy and began licking. On contact, my legs twitched and I orgasmed. She continued licking me as my orgasm shook my entire being.

Once done, Dianne smiled, "I guess you needed to come pretty bad."

My breathing still erratic, I answered, "I didn't know it could feel like that."

She smiled devilishly, "Oh Baby, we are just getting started."

Just as I was about to ask what she meant, she buried her face back between my legs. My clit was sensitive from just having orgasm, and I warned, "Dianne, I can't have multiple orgasms without a lengthy break in-between."

She looked into my eyes and smiled, "Well, I already gave you two."

"Yes," I moaned, "but we had a couple of hours in-between."

Smiling devilishly, Dianne said, "I will take that challenge."

"But, I am too sensitive after I orgasm," I explained.

Dianne ignored my pleas and returned to my pussy. The first few licks were like sharp tingling pains, but after a few long licks from Dianne's tongue and the sensation shifted to sweet tingling pleasure. Within a couple of minutes, I could feel the slight simmering of a future orgasm. Suddenly relaxing, I let go of my sexual insecurities and enjoyed the pleasure my best friend was giving me.

Her tongue roamed all over my pussy and surprised me when she slid lower, and pulling my ass cheeks apart, licked my virgin butthole. Such an act was naughty and sinful and would have been taboo at any other moment of my life, but her tongue teasing me in the forbidden zone somehow made this moment even hotter.

She swirled her tongue on my rosebud before slowly penetrating my ass barely with her tongue. I let out a whimper and she slowly slid her tongue back to my pussy.

When she returned, she increased the pressure on my pussy and finally gave my swollen clit some attention. As my breathing increased, my orgasm beginning to build, she slid a finger in pussy and began pumping slowly. My orgasm continued to build but like often happened, it lingered there in perpetual almost-land, and my frustration began to build too.

I moaned, "Sorry, Dianne, this is what happens. I get to the brink of a second orgasm, but it never breaks through."

She smiled, "Close your eyes, Baby, and trust me."

I obeyed, knowing it wasn't going to happen. I couldn't even give myself multiple orgasms, and believe me, I have tried.

She returned to my pussy and became aggressive as she attempted the impossible. Her fingers, now two in me, felt amazing, as did her mouth on my clit, but still my orgasm eluded me.

Suddenly, out of nowhere, she pulled her fingers out of my pussy and slid a wet finger of hers in my ass.

She began tapping on my clit with her other hand as she fingered my ass. Also out of nowhere she began to talk nasty. "Come for me baby, come like the little lesbian slut you have always wanted to be. You have wanted to be my little lez pet forever, haven't you slut. You are my slut, my pretty lesbian slut. Now come for me, now!"

I couldn't believe it but the mixture of being fingered in my virgin ass, having my clit spanked and being called a slut were three sensations I'd never experienced, that had my mind reeling, my body quaking and my pussy flooding as I reached a second earth quaking orgasm. "Oh my god, fuck, Dianne, it feels so good."

She asked, adding to the orgasmic bliss, "Who owns you, slut?"

I responded without hesitation or thought, "You do Dianne, I am your slut, your fucking lesbian slave." My screams probably could be heard from next door as the most intense pleasure I have ever felt fulfilled me.

When I finally opened my eyes, I was eye to eye with Dianne whose face was shiny with my juice. I have always leaked profusely when I did orgasm and this was even more than usual.

My orgasm subsided, but I still felt twitches in my legs. My body seemed to be forever in bliss.

Dianne stood up and went to her closet. She returned a moment later with something I had never seen before in real life: a strap-on cock. I couldn't imagine Dianne owning one, never mind using one. She said, "Stand up, Baby."

I did, although my knees were still rather weak and I was rather lightheaded. She wrapped the strap-on around my waist and said, "Getting you off got me so horny, I need to get fucked right now."

Looking at her in awe, I pointed out, "I can't even begin to figure out why you own a strap-on."

She smiled devilishly, "Want to hear a secret?"

"Of course," I replied, dying to know everything about my sexy best friend.

"I use it on Candace, regularly," she revealed.

"Candace, our babysitter?" I gasped.

Her smile remained dripping with naughtiness, "The one and only. Since she turned eighteen, she has been my personal plaything."

"No way," I mindlessly babbled.

"Yes, way," she countered. "And, I guarantee she would eagerly be your plaything too. She is completely obedient and loyal, like a trained puppy."

"Oh my God," I said, stunned by yet another shocking twist in the day.

Dianne crawled onto the bed and begged, "Now get over here and shove your cock in me. Fuck your best friend."

Looking at my hot best friend bent over and waiting to be fucked, I suddenly felt my pussy tingle again. I climbed onto the bed, put the long plastic cock at her pussy entrance and rubbed it up and down deciding to tease her a bit. I don't know what happened, but wearing a cock I suddenly had a personality shift and got uncharacteristically controlling.

She moaned and begged, also unlike her, "Please shove it in me, Baby."

I obliged, sliding my long wide cock easily into her wet pussy. Once all the way inside, I held it there, as a long moan escaped her lips. I waited, lodged deep in her pussy for her to beg for more. I didn't have to wait long.

She moaned, "Your cock feels so good in me, Baby."

I slapped her ass, "You love my cock, don't you?"

She looked back at me with a startled smile, but answered, "Hmmm, yes Baby, I love your cock. Now show me how you use it."

I began slowly pumping her pussy with my cock. At first it was slow, deep movements, but as her moans got louder I shifted to fast, hard thrusts, desperately attempting to get deeper than she had ever been fucked. Each deep thrust had her pushed forward as my body crashed into hers.

This hardcore fucking continued for a few minutes before she began bouncing back on me and was soon riding my cock for all it was worth. I grabbed back and held onto my ankles as Dianne pounded herself on my cock.

She screamed, "Aaaaaaaahhhh," as her orgasm ripped through her. She fell forward, my cock sliding out of her and she spun onto her back and began slapping her clit as she orgasmed. Watching her in full sexual bliss had me wet as well and I dove between her legs and licked her delicious pussy again as the juices naturally flowed out of her. Another taste of her heavenly sin and I confirmed my first conclusion that I would be between her legs again and again. It flowed like wine and I wanted the tap to flow forever.

Her orgasm never seemed to end as her moans continued, before she ordered, "Take off your cock, Baby."

I quickly got the harness off me and she pulled me forward, shifting us so are legs were scissored together and our pussies were touching. She then began moving up and down and we were rubbing our pussies together. The sensation was odd and yet so hot as we we're both suddenly using each other's pussy to get each other off, which I would later learn was called tribbing.

Dianne demanded, "I want you to come again for me, Loretta. Be a good pet, come for me, Baby."

Desperate to please her, I began bucking my pussy onto hers. We were in sweet unison. Each up-and-down rub stimulated me in a way I never had felt before, and my inconceivable third straight orgasm, fourth if you include the one a couple of hours ago, began to build and build and build until Dianne demanded, "Come slut, come for your Mistress."

The thought of Dianne as my Mistress was too much and my orgasm exploded out of me in one big wave of exhilaration.

I screamed, "I'm coming."

Dianne screamed back, "Me too, Baby."

And we both collapsed onto our backs, perspiration dripping off our bodies. I lay there in euphoria for a few minutes before Dianne's lips met mine. A sweet gentle kiss that warmed my body, my mind and my heart.

Eventually, we got dressed as Dianne said, "Well, that was better than watching a football game."

I replied, "Agreed. I love this new Super Bowl tradition."

Dianne looked me in the eye, "You know this will be more than just a once a year thing, Baby."

I blushed, "I hope so, Mistress."

"You liked being called a slut," Dianne smiled.

"I know, I can't explain it, but being called names by you really got me off."

"Well," Dianne said, "You are both my best friend and my slut."

"And you are my best friend and my Mistress," I smiled back.

As we walked back to my house, she added, "Next time, I'll invite Candace over. She has wanted to eat your cunt, forever."

I blushed, but nodded in agreement

We entered my house, and my hubby instantly called out, his tone implying his annoyance, "Where have you two been?"

Dianne smiled and said, "We were just dyking out at my house."

My husband laughed, thinking she was kidding, "I would have loved to see that."

I joked back, "Well, shut off the game and we will do it right here."

"Yeah right," he ignored my offer and handed me an empty food tray. "There's only five minutes left."

I looked at the TV. The game was tied.

I went to the kitchen with Dianne and she grabbed a cucumber and said, "Do you have any special sauce left?"

The End